NONI
AND THE GREAT
CHAWWWKLIT
MYSTERY

NONI
AND THE GREAT
CHAWWWKLIT
MYSTERY

Dermot Whelan

ILLUSTRATED BY FINTAN TAITE

Gill Books

Gill Books
Hume Avenue
Park West
Dublin 12
www.gillbooks.ie

Gill Books is an imprint of M.H. Gill & Co.

978 07171 9185 7

Edited by Venetia Gosling
Proofread by Caroline Twomey
Designed by Bartek Janczak
Printed by Clays Ltd, Suffolk

This book is typeset in 12 on 21pt, Minion Pro.

A CIP catalogue record for this book is available
from the British Library.

5 4 3 2 1

MIX
Paper from
responsible sources
FSC® C018072

For Dermot Snr. I know you'd get

a great kick out of this.

And for the wonderful people of Limerick.

MEET THE CHARACTERS

Noni

Limerick's most notorious – ahem, I mean, celebrated – chocolate seller! Never afraid to cut a few pesky corners to make a profit. Even if that means potentially poisoning her customers with her crazy concoctions. Chunks McSturdy's number-one fan.

Francis

Loyal servant to Noni and world's worst guard-bird. Loves a good audiobook.

Seán

Age 10. Big brain, small clothes. Quick with a fact and great with numbers. Loves Noni and making fake sweets.

Emma

Age 12. Hates being bored and loves an adventure. Wishes she had more independence – and wishes Noni would follow stricter health and safety guidelines.

Chunks McSturdy

Munster's finest-ever rugby player. Dashing good looks and incredible sporting ability. A chin you could grate cheese on and great with a machine gun.

Marguerite

Posh pram merchant. Loves anything pink. Also Chunks McSturdy's number-one fan. Noni's archenemy. Appreciates a good-quality welly boot.

Noleeh

A no-nonsense, bagpipe-
playing recluse who knows
her way around a herb
garden and a book of spells.
Very angry with Noni over
something rather disgusting.

Tom

Excellent at making
inventions, terrible at
naming them. Always
ready to lend a hand
and loves a good bowl
of beans.

PROLOGUE

There isn't much light in the cave.

But one crisp shaft of sunlight, entering through a crack in the rock, is enough to illuminate the murky, bubbling mess in the centre of the cave floor.

Steam rises to the roof of the cavern, as the brown, tar-like substance begins to FROTH angrily and spit out over the edges of the pool. A WICKED stench fills the air ...

Darkness falls, engulfing whatever light was struggling to survive in this terrible place. It's going to need more than a good plumber to sort this one out …

CHAPTER 1

'W*HERE* are those little pups?' mumbled the old woman as she **BASHED** her bockety pram off her sitting room furniture. She was attempting to navigate an unholy mess of boxes and packaging that were strewn across the floor of her tiny terraced house.

Her home, nestled in the shadow of Limerick's **Thomond Park stadium,** consisted of one small bedroom, a very messy sitting room and a wardrobe pretending it was a kitchen. No ordinary person would attempt to run a business from such a confined space.

This, however, was no ordinary old woman, and no ordinary pram.

This was **Noni Considine,** the greatest (and most controversial) pram-based chocolate seller in all of Limerick City. And she was in a hurry.

Today was the day of the big match – and big match days were when she made her best money. She'd be outside that rugby stadium selling

sweets,

chocolate and

fizzy drinks to anyone

with a tooth in their head. That would have ruled out half the city when Noni was growing up, but not now. Dentists were much better these days and used far fewer gardening tools to do their job, so her business was booming. Well, it would have been, if her two supposed helpers hadn't been running late again.

'How am I supposed to get all this ready for the SUCKERS – I mean, customers – if I have to do everything by myself?'

Noni ripped the top off a bag and poured what looked like frozen peas out on to the coffee table. **Francis**, her pet raven, was perched in his usual spot on the handle of her pram. He had his mind on more important matters and was wearing headphones (being partial to a self-help podcast or two).

Francis, although a raven, fancied himself as a kind of feathery guard dog. In the cut-and-thrust world of pram-based street vending, security is always advised, and Francis was prepared to challenge anyone brave (or foolish) enough to try to take on Noni. Sure, he was small in stature, but in a tricky situation he could be quite formidable – he had a beak and he knew how to use it.

Unfortunately, he was often so engrossed in his audiobooks and podcasts, he missed most of the action when it went down. Noni had lost count of the number of times an opportunistic hand had reached into the pram and her 'guard-bird' had been mentally somewhere else.

Suddenly, there was a knock at the door, and a young boy's voice called through the letterbox.

'Noni! It's us! We're here!'

'About time!' huffed Noni, continuing to mumble under her breath as she made her way to the door. It was impossible to make out *exactly* what she was saying, but it seemed to include the words 'Perpetual Sacred Heart', some saints' names and she *may* have sworn a few times.

Although the journey to the door was only a few feet, it took her forever to get there with all the clutter in the way.

'Noni, we're here!' said the letterbox again.

'I'm *coming,* ye little ...'

Before she could reach it, the front door burst open and two children fell through it, landing on the door mat in a messy heap. **Emma** and her younger brother, **Seán,** looked up at Noni with matching broad grins.

'What in God's name are ye up to?' Noni cried. 'That's the most dramatic entrance I've seen

since Father O'Riordan fell off the choir balcony last Christmas.'

'Hi, Noni,' came a voice from outside. The children's mum hovered anxiously on the pavement, while their dad waited impatiently in the car. 'Are you sure you're still okay to mind them for the night? I'm sorry it's so last minute but we need to get new stock for the shop, and it'll be so much easier on our own.' They owned an antique store in the centre of town and often had to go to trade shows and markets all over the world. Noni was their nearest neighbour and was used to helping out.

'No problem, off you go, see you then, BYE, BYE,' said Noni, flustered, as she did her best to get rid of them.

'We're still interested in buying that pram of yours, you know, Noni. It's a fabulous antique and worth a few bob, I dare say,' Emma and Seán's father called out from the car hopefully.

'I'm afraid not,' said Noni through gritted teeth, doing her best to be polite. 'It's still NOT FOR SALE.'

'Pity. Anyway, we'll be back tomorrow night to pick them up.'

'Okay, no problem, bye, bye, see you then, safe … antiquing.' Noni was keen to get cracking on her preparations for the match-day sales.

'And Noni,' called the kids' dad, 'no crazy stuff this time, yeah?'

'Of course not, I'll wrap them in cotton wool as always, heh heh. BYE, BYE!' She waved them off at last and turned to go inside. 'Antique! How dare they? That pram is state of the art! Sure, it's only fifty-two years old!'

She slammed the door shut but it swung open again straight away.

'You really have to get that front-door latch fixed, Noni,' said Emma, as she picked her and Seán's overnight bag up off the floor. 'It's been weeks since that angry customer kicked it down and it's not safe.'

'I would ask the locksmith to fix it,' said Noni, 'but the man who kicked it down *is* the locksmith! And I don't know what his problem was, anyway. Those

Easter eggs I gave him were perfect. I thought the broken glass gave them a bit of extra **CRUNCH**.'

Seán laughed and looked around the room with excitement. He thought Noni was hilarious and big match days were his favourite – the excited buzz of the crowds, the **YELLING** and selling and, most of all, the feast of leftover sweets and chocolate at the end of it. He spied the raven on the pram and gave him a wave.

'Hi, Francis!' he said. The bird nodded briefly, then went back to listening intently to his audiobook.

Seán's blond hair was straight and short. He was small for his age, and sometimes that annoyed him. He found he didn't get picked for sports teams much and his mother always had to buy him clothes for kids way younger than his actual age. Most of the other kids at school wore tracksuits and sports clothes and cool trainers, but he preferred smart trousers and shirts. He felt they made him look a bit more grown up and he kind of felt like his dad in them. He loved science and had tons of books on space, rockets,

bridges, nature, you name it. And, if you suddenly needed to know the surface temperature of Jupiter's moon, then he was your man. (It's minus 260 degrees Fahrenheit, by the way. He saw it in a documentary.) He was also pretty good at maths, keeping track of all Noni's pram transactions on an app on his phone. He loved hanging out with Noni, she was always good fun and she never teased him, unlike his sister …

Emma wasn't as keen as her brother on being baby-sat by Noni, or anyone else for that matter. She was only twelve, but she liked to think she was much more mature than other kids. Definitely mature enough to be allowed to stay home by herself, anyway. Emma was an adventurer. She had climbed every tree within a mile of her home and loved to watch survival shows on TV. Her tracksuit bottoms were always covered in grass stains, but her skateboard tricks were coming along nicely and she'd even built a ramp for her roll-erblades. She'd been planning to spend the day trying it out, until her parents had sprung this latest buying trip on her. Selling chocolate from a pram with Noni didn't seem that exciting in comparison.

She sighed and tucked a strand of her long wavy brown hair behind her ear as she looked around.

The floor and furniture of Noni's sitting room were covered with Noni's merchandise. There was everything you'd expect Limerick's finest pram confectionery merchant to have in stock, from choc-olate bars to fizzy drinks, but there were some stranger items there too: tins of vegetables, wom-en's make-up kits and lots and lots of paint. It was probably a good thing that the carpet and furniture were covered in all of this because they, like Noni, had seen better days. One time, Seán had stared too long at the swirly pattern on the carpet, and it had made him so dizzy, he'd thrown up on Noni's couch, though in actual fact, that had only improved it.

'Hurry up,' said Noni, 'you two are late and this pram won't fill itself.'

'Mam and Dad said you have to let us go to bed before midnight. They're worried you're a bad influence,' said Emma, slightly distracted by the messiness of the room.

'A bad influence? HOW DARE THEY? Didn't I teach you how to swim?'

'By pushing us off a bridge,' replied Emma, frowning and folding her arms.

'And didn't I bring you to the zoo last week?' asked Noni.

Seán chuckled. 'That was three donkeys in a field, Noni. And you made us ride them to the supermarket.'

'Well, I can't carry everything. That was my big weekly shop. Anyway, don't I pay you for your work?'

'**No!**' the children said in unison.

'Well, if your parents are that worried, why do they keep asking me to babysit you?'

''Cos you're cheap?' said Seán.

'And don't forget available,' said Noni. 'The most important quality in a childminder. Now, unless you'd prefer to be doing homework, HOP TO IT!', and she waved a bony finger at them.

There was no doubt Noni was a strange-looking woman. You wouldn't necessarily say that she was ugly, because that would be unkind, but when in her company you weren't sure whether to stare or look away. Though her skin was rosy and youthful, Noni had grey facial hair. Emma had given her a voucher for a beauty parlour one birthday to have it removed. Noni, however, thought it made her look distinguished and had swapped the voucher for custard. She also had a rather crooked nose, but that was balanced out by her crooked chin. Her eyes, however, were beautiful. They were deep blue and always sparkled, projecting kindness, mischief and excitement, all rolled into one. Even when she was cross with the children, Noni's eyes seemed to say otherwise. If she was angry with anyone other than Emma and Seán, however – say if someone tried to touch her pram without permission – she had a fierce look that would melt rocks. But when she smiled, it made you want to smile too. On the end of her nose sat a pair of thin, gold-rimmed glasses that she rarely ever actually looked through. She always wore the same faded purple coat and brown headscarf, whether it was the depths of

winter or a scorching summer's day. The children had
never seen her in anything else
and, whenever they tried to
imagine her as a baby, they
pictured her lying in her
pram in the same coat
and scarf. She seemed
to have endless amounts
of energy and, despite
having a slight stoop, she
could really motor when she wanted to.

Noni had been part of the children's lives for as
long as they could remember. In fact, she had been part
of the family since before they were even born. Living
at the end of their street, Noni had even minded their
father, David, when he was young. Seán and Emma's
dad often spoke about all the dinners Noni had made
him when he lost his mother as a teenager. And Seán
and Emma's own mother, Siobhán, often mentioned
how Noni had been one of the first to welcome her to
the neighbourhood when she moved there after her

marriage. Despite Noni's eccentric ways, they all had a soft spot for her – and knew that she enjoyed the children's company, even if she didn't always admit it. If you asked Noni, she'd probably tell you she needed them for one purpose and one purpose only – *to sell chocolate!*

Noni's sales system was pretty much the same for every match. Fill the bottom rack of the pram with the heavy stuff. Fizzy drink cans, boxes of bars and Noni's 'CHANGE STICK'. (When Noni produced the big wooden stick, people rarely stuck around for their change.) Then, the pram itself got filled with the loose stuff – crisps, chocolate bars, packets of sweets and jellies. It was an ancient pram, like you'd see in old, black-and-white photos of babies at the seaside. It had definitely been through the wars and been patched up again on many occasions. It was basically held together with twine, old chewing gum and hope. But those old prams were big and could hold a lot, which meant less running back and forth for Seán and Emma to restock.

As well as the two main pram compartments, there was another, smaller one which was situated under the hood. This was for 'special' sweets. And preparing these special sweets was the children's most important job.

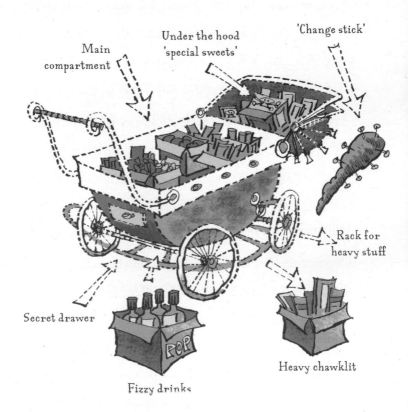

Main compartment

Under the hood 'special sweets'

'Change stick'

Rack for heavy stuff

Secret drawer

Fizzy drinks

Heavy chawklit

'Get working on those peas,' said Noni. 'The nail varnish is over there in that box.'

You see, Noni liked to cut a few corners when it came to her business and anywhere she could make a quick buck she would. She thought confectionery in general was too expensive, and how was she to make a decent profit if the sweets were too dear to buy in the first place? So, Seán and Emma were tasked with creating 'ALTERNATIVE' versions of popular treats, which would then be sold to unsuspecting customers as the real thing. Hence the frozen pea project. The peas were painted with different coloured nail varnish to look like Skittles. Chickpeas were dipped in cold gravy to pass for Maltesers and chew bars were 'reimagined' by picking lumps of chewing gum off the road, sticking them together, then rolling them flat with a rolling pin and putting them in the fridge to harden. As a budding scientist, Seán loved these crazy food inventions and saw the whole thing as one big science experiment. Now his tongue was poking from the corner of his mouth as he sat at the table and concentrated on painting a very tiny pea. Emma was not so convinced and, probably with some justification, was more concerned with the health implications of eating these creations. Noni was a hard taskmaster, though, so Emma continued dipping the chickpeas in gravy.

As well as these homemade versions, there were also some other treats that, at first glance, looked like the real deal but, on closer inspection, would have any concerned citizen backing away from the pram. Noni liked to shop around when it came to her products and she realised that faraway countries you or I have never heard of weren't too bothered by copyright laws and were offering cheaper versions of popular bars online with just a hint of a difference in the name. Instead of a Twix, Noni's version said 'Twox'. Instead of Snickers, she sold 'Nickers'. And a Curly Wurly was now a 'Creepy Crawly'.

If you're a tad concerned right now about those poor unsuspecting sports fans actually getting sick, or even dying, from eating Noni's horrible and very illegal products, then thank goodness for you. Because Noni certainly wasn't concerned about it. Thankfully, most people just spat them out as soon as they bit into them, and if they dared to complain that something wasn't right with their purchase, well, you've guessed it – they met the 'change stick'!

Seán hummed away as he poured the beautifully decorated frozen peas into empty Skittles bags that clearly looked like they'd been rescued from the street. Emma reluctantly packed Nickers bars into the secret pram compartment which, up until this point, no policeman had ever managed to uncover.

'You've got to stop this carry on, you know, Noni,' said Emma. 'Someone is going to get sick. *AGAIN.*'

'I'm not paying you to comment,' replied Noni.

'YOU'RE NOT PAYING ME AT ALL,' said Emma, a withering look on her face.

Noni was too psyched about the big match to take any of Emma's advice on board and continued busily loading the last items into the pram. 'As soon as those cans of Cooka Coola and 6Up are in the pram, we're ready to rock, kids.'

The front door of the tiny house opened directly onto the street and out came the pram, Noni and her two accomplices – I mean, helpers. As Noni used her bubblegum as a temporary lock on the front door, the two children looked up the road at the looming shape of the stadium ahead of them. It was the stadium of dreams – **Thomond Park**. The sun glinted off the shiny curved angles of the stands as thousands of people flooded towards the gates, chattering away excitedly as they passed the children on the doorstep. Smells from food vans selling burgers and hotdogs filled the air and programme sellers shouted above the crowds of spectators, many of whom had already started chanting their team's songs.

'WOW,' said Seán, 'there's nothing quite like match day!' and his eyes lit up with excitement.

'Yeah, yeah, just keep walking,' said Noni, 'there's money to be made, kid, and we're the ones to make it!'

She grabbed the handle of the pram, which had a fully headphoned Francis on it, and off she marched into the fray, with an energy and enthusiasm rarely seen from a woman of … well, that's the thing, no one really knows just how old Noni is.

Noni had had a difficult childhood. Her father worked as an underwater tour guide in the Shannon

Estuary, but only ever managed one day before drowning. As a result, Noni and her seventeen sisters were mostly raised by their mother. Noni also had a brother but to keep things simple, and because the boys' department was another floor up in the department store, her mother dressed him as a girl and called him **Rita.**

The pram business all began with Noni's mother back in the day. She sold odds and ends, this and that, these and those and bits and bobs out of it, until she got a terrible dose of the you-know-whats and was buried in the back of God knows where.

Starting out, Noni sold a variety of things: she sold wares, chairs,

snares, bears,

flares and glares.

There was no real market for any of those things, though, especially the last one, so she finally settled on chocolate. But she pronounced it very differently …

CHAPTER 2

'Crisps here now, boys and girls, get your apples and chaaaawwwwklit!'

Nobody quite knows why Noni goes so posh for only one word in her vocabulary, but that's just how it is. It's as if she's suddenly possessed by the Queen of England just as she attempts to say 'chocolate'. Her lips purse up like a fancy fish and the word seems to get longer every time she says it – 'chaaaaaaaaaaaawwwwwklit'.

'Crisps here now, boys and girls, get your apples and CHAAAAWWWWKLIT!' she cried again, as she stood at her usual spot outside the huge gates of the stadium. Well, that's how she heard it. To everybody else it sounded like, 'cripsernabysagurlap-pasachaaaaawwwwklit!'

She had been shouting the same sentence for so many years, it had lost any real meaning. Whatever she was shouting, it seemed to work. Pretty soon, people were queuing up to buy her wares and the

money started to roll in. Some got the real stuff, other more naive types got the 'alternative' sweets.

A friendly woman in a red Munster jacket appeared.

'Hello, Noni. How are you, love? Hello, kids. A bar and a cola please,' she said with a smile.

'Howya, Bernie,' said Noni, glancing at the children and giving a gentle nod. This was the signal that this customer was to get regular, legal stock.

'You're looking great, Bernie! And how are the family? Is your son still in jail in Siberia …?'

Noni moved off for a proper natter with her old friend. While she was away, a rowdy group of boys approached the pram. The biggest one wore a woolly Munster hat and spoke loudly through a large gap in his front teeth. He was **Conor Delaney,** the school troublemaker, and with him was his usual gang of lads. They were slightly older than Seán and regularly made his life a misery.

'Well, hello, SCIENCE NERD! I see you brought your spaceship along with you. Oh no wait, it's a bockety old pram!'

All the boys laughed, thinking this was hilarious.

'What do you want, Conor?' said Seán.

'*What do you want, Conor*?' repeated the bigger boy in a mock squeaky voice. 'Maybe I want your stupid old pram, Science Boy. Maybe I'll use it to make something decent like a go-kart.' He began to try to pull the pram away from Seán, who held on to it for dear life.

'Let it go!' said Seán, struggling against the strength of the older boy. Suddenly, Francis appeared. He flew into Conor's face and began to peck his cheeks angrily. The older boy let out a yelp of pain.

'**HEY!** Call off your freaky bird!'

'Let go of the pram!' cried Emma, as she came to help her brother.

Conor soon let go out of fear of losing his eyes and began to back away, along with the rest of the gang. He didn't look happy.

'This isn't the end of it, Science Boy! I'll get you *and* that pram!' and he sloped off back into the crowd, clutching the side of his face.

Francis landed back down on the handle.

Noni returned just at that moment. She saw that Seán was a bit upset. 'What happened, Seánie?'

Seán didn't feel like talking about it. 'Nothing, Noni, just … a difficult customer.'

'Well, next time give them some of Noni's "good stuff" and see how *that* goes!'

The sales continued as some got real treats and others got the 'SPECIAL' fare. Noni's reasons for taking a dislike to a customer and deeming them worthy of the homemade treats seemed to vary. She definitely didn't like it if you were rude, or impatient, or spoke with your mouth full. If you took too long to make up your mind, that didn't work either. Other reasons seemed to be more random. One time, Emma saw her give 'liquorice sticks' (green beans dipped in tar) to a man simply because she didn't like his shoes. The worst thing you could do, though, was talk down to Noni. She was a tremendously proud woman – proud of her work, proud of her roots, proud of her city. If you thought you were better than her, you would soon regret it. If you were foolish enough to talk down to her while buying something, then it could be positively LIFE-THREATENING.

Which is where this particular lady went wrong …

A woman approached Noni and the children, wearing a scowl that looked like she would rather be anywhere else but outside Thomond Park on match day. She was wrapped up in a brown fur coat, with a matching brown fur hat on her head, and sunglasses so wide they seemed to take up most of her face. She stood on very high heels and was dragging a man by the shoulder over to the pram. He was a good bit shorter than her and looked sheepish and miserable.

'Get me something to eat, you **imbecile.** If I *have* to go to this barbaric game you'd better make sure I don't have to sit through it on an empty stomach!' She stopped and perused the items on offer in the pram.

'Dear God, what is this **muck?** Would half a lobster be too much to ask for? Why I let you drag me here, I'll never know,' the woman scoffed as she held a handkerchief to her nose, as if the smell of the whole environment was going to make her be sick on the spot. Francis, who up until this point had been lost in his audiobook, suddenly burst into action in his security role and flapped and squawked wildly.

'CALM YOUR FILTHY BIRD!' said the woman, through her handkerchief. Noni's face began to tighten. Her lips became narrower, her eyes smaller and her face took on a very particular red glow – rage. Talking down to her was one thing. Disrespecting the contents of her pram was quite another.

Embarrassed, the man piped up. 'Do you have anything … ahem, that my wife might like? Something a bit more … upmarket?'

Emma, seeing Noni's brewing anger, grabbed her gently by the sleeve in order to lessen the chances of her leaping over the pram and grabbing him by the scruff of the neck.

'Yes!' chimed in Seán, nervously looking at Noni. 'We do. Why not try something from our … DELUXE RANGE? Right, Noni?'

Noni glanced at him and immediately realised what was at play. Her face softened.

'Oh, yes, our DELUXE RANGE. It's brand new for our "special" customers.'

The man looked relieved. Noni patted Francis to calm him down.

'Sounds perfect. Doesn't it, dear?' the man said nervously to his wife.

'Well, it had better be an improvement on the burger I tried to eat a while ago. I've never eaten rotten horse guts, but I imagine that's what they taste like!'

'Oh, yes, you'll love these,' said Noni, reassuringly.

'Which ones?' whispered Seán, as he reached deep into the pram.

'ALL of them,' said Noni, still smiling fakely at the demanding lady.

'*All* of them?' Emma was shocked. 'No one has ever eaten *all* of them at the same time. Is that wise?' she said under her breath.

'I'm sorry, girlie,' said the fur-coat woman, 'who asked *your* opinion? Just give me the damn food before I die of starvation!'

'All of them it is,' said Emma, as what little sympathy she had had drained away fast.

Seán laid out all the 'treats' on the hood of the pram.

'What are they?' snarled the woman.

'Well,' said Noni, pointing to the chickpeas in gravy. 'These are … quail's eggs.'

'Ooh, I *love* quail's eggs,' said the woman, as she scoffed a bunch down. Noni, the children and Francis looked on in amazement.

'And these are coloured … caviar,' said Noni, pointing at the fake Skittles.

'Finally, some food I'm used to,' said the woman as she wolfed down a handful of painted peas. 'Wait a minute!' She grabbed her terrified husband by the arm. 'What's going on here?' Noni and the kids looked at each other worriedly. 'What are you feeding me?'

Emma was just about to crack and apologise when the woman squealed loudly. 'I knew it!' She pointed to the 'recycled' strips of chewing gum. 'French nougat! My absolute favourite!' and she stuffed the lot into her mouth. As she chewed with a very full mouth, her face began to turn red.

'Best give her a drink,' said her husband, growing concerned. 'Got any–'

'Champagne? Sure!' said Seán, as he presented her with a beaker of bubbly liquid they had prepared in Noni's kitchen earlier. Of course, it was the type of rare high-quality champagne you get when you mix mouthwash and washing-up liquid.

The lady grabbed the cup and drank the lot.

'This can't be good,' said Emma, now slightly concerned, as the woman began to look increasingly strange. Her face was turning green and her eyes were BULGING.

'Maybe we should pack up, kids,' said Noni, laughing nervously. Suddenly, the woman let out a high-pitched squeak. And then a growl. And then what sounded like a cat's meow.

'That's new,' said Noni, looking on in shocked amazement.

With her eyes fixed in a strange stare, the woman suddenly assumed the sitting position, as if in an invisible chair, and, with her arms stretched out in front of her, began speaking in a stream of gobbledy-gook so impressive, it would be the envy of any babbling six-month-old baby.

'What is it, dear?' cried her husband, trying to get her attention. Some curious paramedics were passing and now looked on with interest. Suddenly, the woman let out a loud howl like an excited wolf and flopped into a wheelchair the paramedics had with them. She had a peaceful, serene look on her face and was staring at her husband adoringly.

'That's the first time I've seen her smile in twenty years!' he said, with a tear in his eye. 'I don't know what you put in that deluxe range, ma'am, but I'll be coming back for more! I might even get to watch the match in peace now!' And off he went into the stadium pushing his wife along happily, followed by a team of very confused paramedics.

'Will she be okay?' asked Emma.

'Oh, yes,' said Noni confidently. 'I haven't killed anyone yet … haha … in Limerick … so far … this year … that I know of …'

A garda strolled by, eyeing up the trio suspiciously.

'Hello, Emma. Hello, young Seán.'

'Hello, **Garda Ryan,**' they said together, putting on their most innocent-looking faces.

'Was that lady alright?' he asked.

'Oh, yes,' said Noni, 'just another satisfied customer!'

'Very well, but remember, Noni, I'm watching you,'

said Garda Ryan. 'I know all your tricks,' he added, as he disappeared into the crowd.

'Not *all* my tricks, Sergeant Clever Clogs,' said Noni, as she handed another customer a bar marked White Chocolate, which was in fact a bar of old, gone-off milk chocolate that had turned white.

Noni and Garda Ryan had history. Years before, he had arrested Noni for selling multipack items individually. Noni still claimed she was framed and that somebody put the Milky Ways into her pram when she wasn't looking. To this day, whenever she saw the notice: 'Not to be sold separately' written on confectionery she felt sick to her stomach.

As the morning went on, business was booming. Kick-off was 1 p.m. and Noni and the kids were working together like a well-oiled machine. Noni shouted something unintelligible, Emma handled the money and Seán dealt with the sweets. If Noni gave the nod, customers got the real sweets. If she said, 'Take *SPECIAL* care of this customer', then they got the dodgy stuff.

Francis continued to keep an eye out for trouble-makers when his attention allowed. Most of the time, though, he was perched on the pram squawking back affirmations to himself on the instructions of his self-help book. Only Noni could understand raven language, but it was probably the equivalent of 'I AM A CONFIDENT RAVEN. I AM A HAPPY RAVEN. I AM A CREATIVE RAVEN!'

Francis was lost in his headphone world when a homeless man appeared beside the pram. His clothes were dirty and torn and there were holes in his shoes.

'Would you have any old sweets or the like going spare?' he asked, smiling a toothy grin at the children.

'No way, we're always givin' you free stuff!' yelled Noni. 'Away with you – go bother some other hard-working entrepreneur!'

Seán and Emma liked the homeless man, and Emma slipped him a packet of jellies and a fizzy drink while Noni was distracted.

'Thank you, girlie,' he whispered, and off he went about his business.

Just then, a large commotion caught their attention. It seemed there was something happening by a temporary stage erected a short distance away. Someone was causing quite a fuss and drawing excited screams from the crowd. Cameras began to flash.

'Oh, cool! It's Chunks McSturdy!' exclaimed Seán.

Noni immediately fainted and fell backwards on to Seán, who fell backwards on to Emma, who fell backwards on to the pram, sending Francis flying up off the handle.

'Not again,' said Emma. 'Noni, wake up, I'm *SQUASHED!*'

Noni slowly came round and struggled back to her feet. 'He's *such* a dreamboat,' she said sleepily, an utterly smitten look on her face.

Chunks was the hero of the rugby club. He had brought them to more Cup and League finals than any other player in history. Standing at six foot, four inches tall, with a chiselled jaw, shampoo-advert hair and muscles on his muscles, he was the focus of attention for most of the women in the city. *Especially* Noni. She had been to every one of Chunks' big games. She was there when he scored ten tries against Leinster. She was there when he did a triple backwards somersault to score between the posts against Connacht. And she was there when he single-handedly rescued a caterpillar that had wandered on to the pitch during a game against Ulster.

Noni's house was filled with Chunks McSturdy merchandise. She had the Chunks lunchbox, bubble bath and ironing board cover. She even had the official Chunks McSturdy cuckoo clock, where his head popped out of a rugby ball every hour on the hour. Francis didn't like that one much. And here was Chunks, standing just a few feet away from her. She was *STARSTRUCK*.

The children held a box of orange Tic Tacs under Noni's nose to bring her round.

'I'm fine, I'm fine,' said Noni, as she adjusted her headscarf and straightened her glasses. 'I must have eaten something funny earlier.'

'Yeah, sure,' replied Emma, as she and Seán smirked knowingly at each other.

'Tidy up the pram. Francis, fix your feathers. He might come over here looking for some chawklit and I want to be ready. I'll get his attention.' Jamming two fingers into her mouth, she attempted a whistle, but mostly managed to spit all over Seán and Emma, who recoiled in disgust. 'He can't hear me. Kids, run up there and ...' She stopped short when she spotted someone talking to Chunks McSturdy beside the stage.

'WHO DOES THAT WAGON THINK SHE IS?' hissed Noni.

Leaning her hand on Chunks' shoulder, throwing her head back and laughing wildly at him, was none other than **Marguerite Shannon,** Noni's archenemy. She too sold chocolate from a pram but was part of a new, younger generation of sweet merchants. Her pram was a fancy modern Bugaboo and, unlike Noni's pram's wheels, hers were fully round. Feeling Noni's wares were old-fashioned, Marguerite sold a more contemporary range of products, like organic chocolate, handmade energy balls, health bars and protein shakes. She didn't wear a headscarf like the older women. Instead, she showed off her long, platinum-blonde hair with yellow streaks, all tied up with a pink scrunchy. In fact, everything she wore was pink, right down to her designer welly boots. She was always seen chatting to the players from the team.

Noni was incensed. 'Look at her, she thinks she's so great, laughing at his jokes. She hasn't even seen a game in years. The closest she gets to a match is lighting the fire! Hey, Marguerite! Your hair is lovely. Did you knit it yourself?'

'Stop it, Noni,' said Emma, pulling her away from the stage area.

Marguerite looked over, frowned for a minute, and then howled even louder at Chunks' jokes, all the while fixing her gaze on Noni.

'She is a piece of work,' said Noni, scowling.

Just then, a microphone squealed and a short, stocky man in a suit appeared, smoking a cigar. He reached up to grab the microphone but was too short so someone else had to hand it down to him.

'Ahem,' he said, 'can I have your attention, please. We'd like to invite up someone very special to say a few words ahead of the big rugby match today. Would you please welcome the captain of the Munster rugby team, Chunks McSturdy!'

The crowd went wild. All the local newspapers and TV and radio reporters were there to catch the action. Chunks took to the stage and waved at his fans.

'Hi everyone. I'm Chunks McSturdy!' he said.

This time Emma and Seán were ready, and propped Noni up with their arms.

'And I'm here today to announce our new sponsor: **TOTES PROTES PROTEIN BARS!** They only taste a bit like sawdust! And I'm also delighted to say that Marguerite Shannon is our main sales agent for **Totes Protes Protein Bars.** So, if you want one, just pop over to her state-of-the-art pram. Enjoy the game, folks!'

Chunks stepped down off the stage and began posing for photos.

'Look at her,' said Noni in disgust. 'She thinks she's so great with her **fancy sweets.** I sold **protein bars** long before her, you know.'

'Wasn't that just a strip of bacon sellotaped onto a

Mars Bar?' asked Emma.

'Well, yes, but it filled you up. There's great rough-age in Sellotape.'

'C'mon, let's sell some more chocolate, the crowd will be going in for the match soon,' said Seán.

The thought of money seemed to snap Noni out of her mood and she got her game face on.

'ABOY DA KID,' she said, which was a Limerick term that seemed to mean 'okay', 'hello', 'well done', 'how are you?' and five hundred other things.

Just then, the small man with the cigar who had been on stage approached the trio.

'Noni Considine?' he said, putting out his hand. 'Gerry Madden from the County Council.'

Noni reluctantly shook his hand. 'Take *SPECIAL* care of this customer please, kids.'

'I'm okay for frozen peas in nail varnish, thank you very much, children,' said Gerry, smirking.

'Are you here to make me pay tax?' shouted Noni. 'I paid my tax for the year, every cent of it!'

'Yes, but that was in 1978. You haven't paid a penny

since, Noni. But I'm not here to talk about tax. I'm here about something even more important.'

Noni softened a bit. 'What is it?'

'I need you to come with me.'

'Now? But this is my prime retail opportunity!'

'**NOW**,' replied Gerry sternly.

Noni huffed, lifted the headphones off Francis' head momentarily and shouted into his ear. 'Francis, **guard the pram with your life!** If I'm not back in ten minutes, call the police immed ...' Realising her already strained relationship with the law, she reconsidered. 'Actually, if I'm not back in ten minutes, just wait another ten minutes.'

Francis put one wing up to his head in a salute and Gerry led Noni and the children away from the bustling crowd.

'Fine, but I'm invoicing the council for lost business.'

'Noni, if we don't do something about this, you may not *have* a business.'

CHAPTER 3

Gerry puffed on his cigar while he led Noni and the children towards the rear of the stadium, away from the excited rugby fans. They continued until they reached a little turnstile they had never seen before.

'Through here,' he said.

Noni hesitated.

'I'm *not* the taxman, Noni.'

'Fair enough, kid,' said Noni as they pushed on through and headed down a staircase. The steps went down and

       down and

              down, and their footsteps echoed in the increasing darkness.

Seán became uneasy and moved closer to his sister. 'Er, guys, where are we going? I'm not too comfortable about dark basements,' he said nervously.

'Yeah, where *are* we going? I'm going to bill you for a new hip if you keep this up,' said Noni, shaking her head at the man from the council.

'Nearly there,' said Gerry, as he led them down the last few steps and pushed open a small wooden door. The door had writing on it, but it was in a language neither Seán nor Emma recognised. Inside was a dark room, with just pockets of light here and there. It took the gang a while for their eyes to adjust.

When they did, they saw that the room was actually very big, with forklifts abandoned to one side, and conveyor belts lying idle. Whatever usually happened in here, it wasn't happening now.

Just then, they heard a commotion coming from

behind one of the large machines. It sounded like two cats fighting, and boxes were getting knocked over in the scuffle.

As Noni and the kids approached, they saw something truly strange. Standing around the scattered boxes was a group of five tiny people, pushing and shoving each other. No more than two foot high, they looked like babies, but with grown-up faces. They had soft downy hair on their heads, and quite pronounced stubble on their faces. One even had a beard. They were all wearing overalls and shouting in high-pitched voices. Just then, the bearded fellow wrestled one of the others to the ground. Playing cards and jellybeans were scattered all over the ground as the rest of them egged the two on.

Emma and Seán's mouths dropped open in amazement.

'WHO ARE THEY?' gasped Emma.

'Stop this at once, ye reprobates! I'll have ye back stealing socks from tumble dryers if you don't quit this instant!' shouted Gerry, as he stooped to pull the wrestlers apart. Clearly he had some authority here, and the little people quickly snapped to attention.

The bearded one who'd started the fight dusted himself off and stepped forward, speaking quickly and pointing at the others, who soon joined in.

'Elra kanay tapolo thrinsta laya manu gregalle!'

'What are they saying?' asked Noni, perplexed. She began to speak loudly and slowly to the strange little creatures. 'Are you from Caherdavin?'

'English, please, we have guests,' said Gerry to the little folk.

'The game was going fine until *he* started cheating,' repeated the bearded one, pointing at the one he'd been fighting. Now the kids could see him, they noticed his moustache and ear protectors.

'And he stole our jellybeans,' piped up one of the others.

'I don't care one bit about your shenanigans,' said Gerry. 'Now, calm yourselves, because I've brought some very important guests to meet the lot of you.'

'Sorry, Gerry,' said the smallest of the group.

'Yes, sorry, Gerry,' echoed the others.

'Right so, let me introduce you. This here is **Aonghus,** the supervisor.'

A bearded Aonghus stood with his hands in the pockets of his overalls, still clearly put out about the scuffle. He gave a half-hearted hello.

'And this is **Fionn,** the shop steward.'

Fionn tweaked the curly corner of one side of his moustache. 'A pleasure.'

'Then these are the machine operators: **Aidan, Olan** and **Bran.**'

'**Aboy da kid,**' said Bran, while the other two just stared.

'Now, these people' – Ger nodded towards Noni and the kids – 'are our guests. Hopefully, they will be able to help us with our ... problem. Bring them to the pool.'

The tiny people led the way out of the room and down a maze of corridors lit by fluorescent bulbs, some of which flickered and BUZZED. It was damp and musty and Seán and Emma were clearly confused.

'What *is* this place? It smells like a mixture of school and hospital,' said Seán, creasing up his nose.

'And what are those little people doing here?' said Emma. 'Are we still under the stadium?'

'Does anyone know the score in the match?' asked Noni. 'Did Chunks score?' She seemed utterly unfazed by the whole experience.

They arrived at a great rusty metal door. Bran started opening a very complex system of locks, pulling handles and turning metal wheels embedded in the door.

'You're about to see what has been known for thousands of years as the **Chocolate Spring**,' said Gerry. 'And these creatures are its keepers. They are a very ancient tribe of fairies, sworn to protect and manage this special place.'

'FAIRIES?' asked Seán, surprised. 'But they don't have pointy ears.'

'Or wings,' added Emma, clearly confused. 'Or pointy shoes, or nice clothes. They're all wearing … boiler suits.'

'Hey!' piped up Aonghus. 'Not all fairies have pointy ears or wings, you know. That's a common stereotype that we find offensive. But we do all have feelings!'

'*I* have pointy ears,' said Fionn, taking off his ear protectors and preening them.

'And you think you're SO great, don't you? Pity they didn't come with manners, you cheat!'

The fairies started to grapple again, yelling at each other in their own language once more.

'That must be the strange language that's written on the door back there,' said Seán, pleased with himself for working it out.

'It is,' replied Gerry, 'and just as well you can't understand it, 'cos they're not saying particularly flattering things to each other, if you get my meaning.'

He turned to the scrapping fairies and yelled. 'Knock it off or I'll clip you around the ear, pointy or not!'

There was a loud metallic **CLUNK** and Bran, Olan and Aidan joined forces to push the great rusty door, which began to slowly groan and squeal its way open.

It was very dark inside, even darker than the last room. Olan struck a match and lit a torch on the wall. Lifting it from its holder, he bent down and touched the torch to the floor in front of them. With a **WHOOSH,** a line of blue fire spread like a spider's web through cavities in the floor. Blue flames ignited on torches all along the walls. At last they could make out their surroundings. They were in a rocky cavern. The air was cool, but the smell was strong. In the centre of the room was a large pool of what looked like black water. As they approached it, they could see that the liquid was thick and bubbling and it gurgled away while making some really rather disgusting fart noises.

'Sounds like you after a bucket of chicken, Noni,' said Seán.

'How dare you!' said Noni. 'I'm only like that after garlic and cheese chips.'

'That's gross,' said Emma, who was finding it hard to look at the pool. 'Is that … chocolate?'

'Yes, it is. This is the Chocolate Spring,' said Gerry, 'a place of terrific importance. Or rather, it was. For thousands of years, all of the kingdom's chocolate has bubbled up through this hidden pool. Every chocolate bar in Ireland has come from this sacred place and been tasted by royalty and paupers alike. All the great kings of our time have come here at important moments to gain wisdom, inspiration and ... well, chocolate. It is even said that the ancient hero of Irish legend, the great warrior **BrianBorú**, came here on the eve of a great battle with his enemies. He had a special sword fashioned by the fairies from the purest chocolate at this very spot, which he then took into the fierce battle.'

'Did he win?' asked Seán, enthralled by the tale.

'No, the chocolate sword was entirely useless and he was killed pretty much instantly,' replied Gerry.

'Haha! What a tulip,' said Noni, laughing.

'Yeah, that wasn't our finest hour,' said Fionn sheepishly.

'That's not the story of BrianBorú I was taught in school,' said Emma, looking dubious.

'They don't teach you this in school because not

everyone knows about it. The chocolate spring has always been kept a secret and only a select few have ever been shown its actual location,' said Gerry.

Aidan chimed in. 'We used to turn the chocolate into all kinds of bars down here. We'd package them up and ship them out. Then we'd wait for all the children to eat it.'

'And for their teeth to fall out,' said Olan. 'Then we'd go up and collect them. But children's diets are too healthy these days, so we don't collect as many teeth. Instead, we sell chocolate to stressed-out mums and dads who eat it after they've put the kids to bed.'

'And then *their* teeth fall out!' the two fairies said in unison, as they high-fived each other. Or, low-fived, given how small they were.

'I like your business style!' said Noni, clearly impressed. 'You should come and work for me! Unpaid work experience, of course.'

'If it's the **finest and purest chocolate** in all the land, then why does it look and smell so **disgusting?**' asked Emma.

'Because it has been **POISONED** by someone, or something,' replied Gerry, as he shook his head sadly and placed the stump of his well-chewed cigar back in his mouth.

Noni reached into the bubbling liquid, scooped up a handful of gloop and shoved it into her pocket.

'What are you *doing*?' exclaimed Gerry. 'Noni, that's highly toxic! Didn't you hear me? This is an emergency. The pool of chocolate has been *poisoned*!'

'I've sold worse in my pram, to be honest.'

'She has,' agreed Emma and Seán in unison.

'And there's a catatonic woman in a furry hat at the match who will prove it,' said Noni, as she scooped another handful of the toxic chocolate into her coat. '**Liquid gold,**' she said under her breath.

'Noni, if you give that to people they might die!' cried Bran.

Noni pondered for a moment. 'They *might* die. Which means they also *might not* die. That's good enough for me.' She took another scoop and, realising her own pockets were now full of chocolatey goo, put

it in the hood of Emma's hoodie.

'Noni!' cried Emma.

Gerry grabbed Noni by the arms and spoke directly to her. 'Noni, if everyone dies from eating this contaminated chocolate, there will be no one left to buy any more chocolate and then, dear woman, *you* will be out of business!'

Finally, the penny dropped.

'Sacred Heart and Lord Almighty and all the saints of heavens above and the soul of Saint Alfonso of Minecraft, why didn't you *say* that? My precious chaaaaawwwwklit! We have to do something!'

'But what *can* we do?' said Aonghus. 'This looks like some kind of BLACK MAGIC.'

'Ha,' chuckled Seán. 'Black Magic is actually a type of choc—'

'Not now, Seán!' interrupted Noni. 'This is no time for confectionery-based coincidences. We need to uncover what mysterious magic is behind all this and save my chaaaawwwwklit business.'

'That's the problem, Noni,' said Gerry. 'I don't know the faintest thing about dark magic – or any kind of magic, for that matter. I fix potholes in the road and get zebra crossings painted outside schools. It's above my pay grade. And these little fellas,' he said, gesturing to the fairies, 'all they know is how to make chocolate bars and gamble for jellybeans.'

'Hey! That's not fair!' said Aonghus in disgust. 'We also gamble for wine gums.'

'But Noni,' said Gerry tentatively, fidgeting nervously with the end of his tie, 'there *is* one person who could possibly help us with all this magic stuff …'

It took a moment for what Gerry was getting at to register with Noni. 'Oh, no. No way! That is not going to happen,' cried Noni. 'There's more chance of me marrying Marguerite Shannon in the morning than doing that!'

Noni began pacing up and down the cavern.

'What is it, Noni? Do what?' asked Emma, perplexed.

'Never mind, 'cos it's not going to happen,' Noni protested.

'Gerry?' asked Emma again.

'Well, you see, Noni has a sister—'

'*HAD* a sister!' interjected Noni.

'A sister who is familiar with the workings of magic and who—'

'Who I haven't spoken to in …' Noni counted quickly on her bony fingers, 'fifteen years!'

'But Noni,' pleaded Gerry, 'Noeleen's the only one who understands this stuff. And if we don't get help now to fix this chocolate problem, we are all in **BIG, BIG TROUBLE.** People could get sick from this poisoned chocolate, like *really* sick. You'll lose your business and I'll lose my career because the most important chocolate supply in the history of Ireland will disappear on my watch! Not to mention what will happen to the fairies!'

The five fairies were now huddled together, whimpering and putting on their saddest faces in an attempt to convince Noni to go along with Gerry's suggestion.

'You're our only hope, dear Noni … *cough … cough*,' said Bran.

'What will become of us?' said Aidan, in the shakiest voice he could muster.

'It's so … COLD,' whined Fionn, looking like he was about to faint.

'Okay, lads, tone down the dramatics, the Oscar's in the bag,' said Gerry.

Noni continued to pace, becoming more hunched under the pressure of it all.

Seán grabbed Noni gently by the sleeve. 'Come on, Noni, this is important. I didn't want to come down to this creepy place, but I did, even though I was frightened. The least you can do is face your sister.'

'Yes, Noni,' added Emma. 'The people of Limerick – of Ireland – need you now. Your sister could be the answer to all of this. I understand that you don't get on, but surely you can put that to one side for something like this?'

Noni looked at Emma's hopeful face in the flickering light, then slumped down on a large rock with a sigh.

'I suppose you're right,' she said, shaking her head. 'My chawklit business is all I have, and the people

71

of Limerick have been so good to me over the years. I owe it to them to try to save their money. I mean, lives.'

The fairies perked up immediately and Gerry began to grin. 'So, you'll do it? You'll ask Noeleen to help us?'

'I will,' said Noni, 'but it's in and out and I'm not making up with her, not after what she did.' Noni sniffed and appeared to wobble. Emma put her arm around her.

'This family stuff is really hard for you, isn't it, Noni?'

'No,' replied Noni with a wince, 'this is the most uncomfortable rock I've ever sat on. Now, let's get out of here before Francis sells my pram for birdseed.'

The gang exited the stadium through the turnstile once more and joined the bustling crowd.

When they had disappeared out of sight, another figure emerged from below the stadium, looking around nervously. Their face was hidden with a hoodie but poking out from underneath were some strands of bleached blonde hair. And, on their feet, was a pair of bright pink wellies …

CHAPTER 4

How much further, Noni? I'm wrecked,' moaned Emma.

'Yeah, Noni, my butt went numb five miles back,' said Seán, wincing. Despite his discomfort, another one of his favourite facts came to mind. 'Did you know, donkeys have amazing memories and can remember other donkeys from over twenty-five years ago?'

'It feels like we've been riding on these ones for twenty-five years,' said Emma, with a groan.

They had left the hustle and bustle of Limerick on

match day far behind them and were now riding donkeys along a path in the woods. Noni's pram had been
attached to her animal and was being towed along
behind by a rope, Francis still perched happily on the
handlebar.

'Hold yer whisht,' said Noni, 'we're nearly there.'

'Are you sure the farmer didn't mind us taking his donkeys?' asked Emma. 'From what Seán and I could see from the gate, he didn't look too happy. He seemed to be shouting a lot.'

'And waving a stick around,' added Seán.

'Of course he didn't mind,' said Noni, 'he *insisted* we borrow them. Sure, he's an old friend. Me and Mr … Farmer go back years.'

'The farmer's name is Mr Farmer?' asked Seán, as he and Emma looked at each other dubiously.

'Look, the donkeys will be back in no time at all, so don't you worry your little heads. My God, the two of you are moaning more than Marguerite did when I hid a gerbil in her pram. I've never seen anyone jump that high. She would have qualified for the Olympics,' she said with a cackle.

'I was thinking, Noni …' said Seán.

'Careful, you could do yourself an injury,' Noni said sarcastically.

'Why don't you like Marguerite?'

Noni's demeanour immediately changed and her posture stiffened.

'Because ... SHE STOLE MY BOYFRIEND,' she said sternly.

'Your boyfriend?' asked Emma, 'I didn't know you had one.'

Noni sniffed and adjusted her headscarf. 'I did. When I was younger. Marguerite grew up on our street. She is a lot ... I mean, *slightly* younger than me, so we never hung around together. She always thought she was better than me. She grew up never having to lift a finger. She has never known real hardship, like I have. The toughest thing she ever had to deal with was getting a paper cut from a fresh fifty euro note! Her parents owned a left-sock factory in town and she never wanted for anything.'

'Except maybe right socks,' said Seán, and he and Emma chuckled secretly.

Noni, though, was lost in her jealous rant.

'She'd saunter into town on a Saturday and stand outside Todds' department store thinking she was all that, when in reality she wasn't even half that. All the boys loved her blonde hair. Back then the only blonde in town was a golden retriever called Minty. So, they all *loved* Marguerite. That's when she stole my boyfriend.'

'What was he like?' asked Emma.

'Oh, he was a DREAMBOAT,' said Noni, with a faraway look in her eyes. 'He was six foot, 32 inches tall. He had all his own teeth and nostrils. He was funny and clever. He could count from one to a hundred forwards, backwards *and* sideways. He had a very important job making all the commas for the local newspaper. One day, after our first kiss behind the printing press, he said he would marry me and we'd move to New York and become chawklit sellers to the stars. Can you imagine it? Selling Tom Cruise a Tiffin or Matt Damon a Mars Bar? "Here you go, Mr Cruise, here's your Tiffin. That'll be five euro fifty. No, I don't have change, sorry. Well, it's early in the day, I haven't had a lot of customers yet. Well, I'm sorry you feel that way, but I can't give you change of your tenner. If you don't like it, why don't you go down the road to the supermarket, they'll sort you out, YOU UNGRATEFUL SWINE! Get away from my pram or I'll call the guards!'"

Even Noni's fantasies about selling chocolate ended in arguments and she had worked herself into a right old state about this one. As her security guard, Francis was also caught up in the fantasy and began flapping about wildly.

'Calm down, Noni! Francis! It's not real! Tom Cruise isn't here!' Emma leaned across and grabbed the old woman's arm, trying her best to relax her. Noni struggled but her breath eventually slowed, and she began to calm herself. Now she just seemed a bit sad. Her head dropped low.

'And then Marguerite came along. She was young and bored and got jealous of my exciting lifestyle. She saw that I had it all – a fast pram, a gorgeous boyfriend, all the chawklit anyone could wish for. And she wanted a piece of the action. So, she got her own new fancier pram with her parents' money and filled it with

posh chocolate. She started to take my business. And, finally, she took my boyfriend.'

'You poor thing, Noni,' said Emma, though she couldn't think of anything worse than having a boy-friend. 'What happened?'

'I called in to see him one day at the newspaper. I caught him and Marguerite kissing at the newspaper office. I was so shocked I knocked over a box of full stops. Just like that he was gone from me forever. I never made it to New York. And I never got to sell chawklit to Tom Cruise.'

'Just as well,' said Seán under his breath. 'Eating it would have been his most impossible mission yet.'

'Did they stay together?' asked Emma.

'Not at all. Marguerite broke up with him two weeks later. She only did it to make me jealous.' She let out a deep sigh.

'It's okay, Noni. It's all in the past,' said Emma kindly. 'You still have us and we think you're great. Even if you *do* make us paint old shirt buttons and sell them as Smarties.'

'Ah, thank you, dear girl. You're so good to me. You two deserve every cent of your wages.'

'You don't pay us, Noni,' Emma reminded her with a smile.

'Yeah, about that, Noni,' said Seán, 'I've been meaning to discuss our lack of wages—'

'HOLD THAT THOUGHT!' said Noni abruptly, stopping her donkey. 'We're here!'

Emma and Seán slid off their animals with a great sense of relief.

Amazingly, Noni rolled off her donkey backwards and landed perfectly upright. It was an astounding feat for a woman of her advanced years, or for anyone for that matter. The kids were stunned.

'Where did you learn to do that?' gasped Seán.

'Off a western on the telly. Now, we'd better get rid of these fellas.' She leaned in and put her face right up to the donkey's ear as if she were about to speak into it.

'Are you a donkey whisperer?' asked Emma, a look of admiration on her face. 'Can you really communicate with them?'

'God, no. I left my mobile in there for safe-keeping,' replied Noni, as she pulled her iPhone from the poor animal's ear. 'AWAY WITH YE, NOW, YE LONG-EARED LUMPS!' With a light smack on one donkey's behind, she set the animals off in the direction of home.

Noni looked around to get her bearings. They were far from the city and deep in the forest. A crow **CAWED** in the treetops above their heads and Francis looked up inquisitively, as if there was a chance he might know him. The wind blew through the swaying branches and there was a chill in the air as the thick foliage kept most of the sunlight out.

Emma zipped up her hoodie to keep out the cold.

'Hmmm …' said Noni. She leaned into the pram and grabbed a chew bar. Undoing the wrapper, she licked it once and then held it aloft into the breeze. She looked around, adjusted her position and licked it again. 'We need to go … over there!' She spun around and pointed at a thicket of trees that looked even denser than the one they were standing in.

'Are you *sure* your sister lives around here, Noni?' asked Emma, as they approached the line of trees. 'It doesn't look like anyone has ever come—'

Suddenly Noni grabbed the two children. 'Wait!' she said urgently. 'Traps …' The three of them stayed rooted to the spot as Noni reached carefully into her pram and took out a bar of chocolate. She went to toss it ahead of her but paused for a second. She swapped it for a different bar.

'I'd better not waste a good one. I'll use a raisin-and-biscuit one instead. They're rotten. I don't know how anyone could put raisins in chocolate. They look like dead flies.' Gently, she threw the bar about six feet ahead of her. As soon as it hit the ground, the earth gave way and a large pit opened up.

Seán and Emma jumped back in shock. When they peered into the pit, they could see sharp wooden spikes pointing upwards and the skeleton of some poor unfortunate trapped on one of them, the ragged remains of a football jersey snagged on his bony torso.

'Oh my God. The poor fellow. What an awful way to go,' said Emma, her hand over her mouth. She pulled Seán closer to her.

'I know,' said Noni, staring into the hole, 'that's a Mayo jersey. As if life wasn't hard enough. It's fairly obvious my sister doesn't like visitors. So, follow directly behind me. Walk where I walk and whatever you do, *don't touch anything*. Francis, guard the pram.'

'Is he not coming?' asked Seán.

'No,' said Noni, 'Francis won't go any further than here. He's no fonder of my sister than I am.'

Francis squawked in agreement, and Noni and the kids moved cautiously off into the trees. They stepped from twig to twig and rock to rock. Despite her years, Noni seemed incredibly nimble.

They carried on deeper into the forest, the children gingerly stepping exactly where Noni went. As the wind blew through the trees above, a shaft of sunlight temporarily blinded Emma. She lost her balance. Stretching out a hand to steady herself, she pushed on a mossy stone that was jutting out from a bush. Suddenly, they heard the sound of chains moving.

'DUCK!' cried Noni, as she fell to the forest floor. A **huge blade,** about the size of a kitchen table, came BURSTING through the branches to their left. It was heading straight for them.

The children dove to the ground just as the terrifying blade swung over their heads and slammed into the trunk of the tree beside them with a ferocious **CLANG.**

They all felt the breeze on their heads as it missed them by inches.

The three of them lay there motionless for a moment. Stunned at their lucky escape, Emma looked up at Seán, who was lying on top of her. He still had his eyes closed tightly in panic.

'Seán, Seán, it's okay. We're okay.'

Seán slowly opened his eyes.

'Don't worry about me, I'm fine,' said Noni sarcastically, as she brushed the leaves off her bum and slowly got to her feet.

'Why couldn't you just take us somewhere normal, Noni, like the cinema?' said Emma.

'I'd settle for the back garden!' said Seán, as he put his hands to his head to check it was still on his shoulders.

'Relax, it missed ye, didn't it? And I told ye not to touch anything, tut, tut.'

Dusting themselves off, the children followed Noni through the very thick undergrowth, with branches and brambles jabbing and poking at them as they went.

Thankfully, they soon saw some more light up ahead as the foliage began to thin out. They stumbled out of the tree line and into a perfectly round little meadow, covered with beautiful wildflowers that gave off the most fantastic smell.

'WOW!' said Seán, 'I like this place.'

A gentle breeze made the flowers dance and sway,

and the sun shone brightly down from above. Birds and other small creatures moved about, seemingly unbothered by the presence of the adventurers.

'This place is wonderful,' said Emma, as she petted a squirrel who had come over to say hello.

'Try not to disturb anything,' said Noni, 'the owner is very particular.'

'Your sister?' asked Seán. 'I can see why she lives here, this place is fantastic. But where's her house?'

'Follow me,' said Noni, moving towards something standing in the middle of the clearing.

As they drew closer, they could see it was a **large grey mushroom.** Like, huge. It was about the size of a wheelie bin and had bright yellow spots on its top.

'Here we go,' said Noni. 'Let's hope she hasn't booby-trapped this as well. Don't just stand there gawking like a couple of drunks outside the chipper, kids, gimme a hand!'

She began unscrewing the top of the great mushroom, which, it quickly became apparent, was actually made of painted metal. It **SQUEAKED** and **GROANED** as Noni slowly turned the top like a wheel.

The other two joined in and, using their combined body weight, together they twisted the heavy lid off the mushroom. It fell onto the grass with a hollow thud.

Three heads peered into the cavity inside.

'Is this some kind of a chimney?' asked Seán.

'Or a secret passage?' said Emma hopefully.

'This is the fun part,' said Noni, with a twinkle in her eye. She lifted up her skirt and coat and clambered up on to the rim of the decapitated fungus. 'Last one in is an egg sandwich!'

As she flicked back the end of her headscarf, she slipped off the side and disappeared down the chute.

The children looked at each other, aghast. Then they looked excited.

They jostled each other to get to the mushroom slide. Emma was there first and jumped up on to the rim.

'Looks like you're the egg sandwich, bro!' she cried, and down she went with a 'WHEEEEE!' that echoed back up the tunnel.

'I quite like egg sandwiches,' mused Seán, then followed his sister.

'WoooooAAAAHHHH!'

FLUMP!

SKLUMP!

FLANUMPH!

Noni and the two children came flying out of the end of the mushroom tunnel to land on some very dusty bags of grain and flour. A cloud of dust filled the air and they coughed until their lungs were clear. They peered around at their surroundings as they waited for their eyes to adjust to the dim light.

'Where are we, Noni?' asked Seán.

'Is this your sister's house?' inquired Emma. 'Hasn't she ever heard of a vacuum cleaner?' She waved the dust away from her face with her hand and coughed.

As he got to his feet, Seán sniffed the air. Somebody was cooking onions and garlic. His stomach grumbled loudly. 'I think I smell … lunch!'

'Good. That means she's home,' said Noni.

They moved from the storeroom out into the main

room of what looked like a cosy cottage. A fire was lit in the hearth and a pot bubbled over it. Some laundry hung drying by the fireplace and a grey cat snoozed on a rocking chair, clearly not bothered at all by the new arrivals.

'What are these?' Seán asked. He was peering into a large jar of greenish liquid that had some kind of mouse-like creature in it. The table was covered in vessels of different sizes, each with a strange specimen floating inside. There were jars of various powders laid out beside bowls of seeds, and bunches of herbs tied with string and ribbon hung from the ceiling.

'I wouldn't touch any of that, my man,' said Noni, and she made the gesture of someone choking painfully.

Seán took a step away from the table.

Emma was looking at old, faded photos on the wall. There were black-and-white pictures of rugby players celebrating with crowds of people. Her attention was drawn to a photo of a girl holding a trophy and laughing.

'Noni, *you're* here!' said Emma excitedly.

Noni peered at the picture, brushing cobwebs off its frame.

'See? It's you, Noni, when you were younger.'

'It does look like me, alright. But that's not me, kid. That's—'

The door burst open so hard it nearly flew off its hinges.

Noni jumped in front of the children to shield them.

A figure stood in the doorway, **HUFFING** and **PANTING.**

'I don't know who ye are or what ye want,' said a shrill voice, 'but PREPARE TO MEET YOUR END!'

Suddenly, the most awful noise filled the air. It was deafening and very high-pitched. Noni, Seán and Emma dropped to their knees and covered their ears. It was like a hundred pigs being squeezed in a vice at the same time, mixed with fingernails on a blackboard and an ambulance siren. It was, without doubt … the worst bagpipe-playing any human being had ever heard.

'Noeleen! Noeleen! It's me, Noni!' She raised one hand up towards the source of the awful sound, the other still cradling her ear. The cat shrieked and ran to hide under the table.

'My ears!' screamed Emma.

Just as the children felt their own ear drums would burst, the squealing stopped.

'Noni? What in God's name are you doing lying on my floor?' asked the silhouette. 'And who are these dirty urchins?'

The two children slowly got to their feet.

'Kids,' said Noni with a sigh, 'meet **Mrs Noeleen Ogarty** … my sister.'

CHAPTER 5

'This is delicious!' said Seán, as he shovelled a spoonful of stew into his mouth.

'I know!' said Emma, also stuffing her face. Noeleen was over at the fireplace, putting more food into a bowl. Emma gently nudged Noni with her elbow and whispered to her.

'Your sister doesn't seem too bad, Noni. She makes a good lunch.'

Noni eyed Noeleen from the table. 'Don't be fooled by a bit of stew, love,' said Noni quietly, 'it'll take more than that to make up for what she did.'

'What did she do to you?' asked Emma.

'Not to me,' replied Noni sadly.

'Don't you know it's rude to whisper?' said Noeleen, interrupting them as she plonked a bowl in front of Noni roughly. She looked at Seán, who was practically eating the bowl itself. 'Don't you ever feed this lot? They look like they haven't eaten in a week.'

'I gave them two bags of jellies for elevenses,' said Noni defensively, 'and sure there's little fried eggs in them packets too.'

Seán chuckled. 'And some of the jellies were green,' he added, 'so I guess we're getting our vegetables too, eh, Noni?' He stuffed a lump of bread into his mouth and grinned at Emma.

'Exactly,' said Noni as she poured some Maltesers on to a slice of bread.

Noeleen sat at the other end of the table and eyed up her visitors. She looked very like Noni but a little more symmetrical. She had a well-defined nose, thin lips and an intense stare. She was also slightly younger than Noni and you could tell she had been very pretty in her youth. She didn't wear a headscarf and her hair was long, white and very straight, reaching all the way down to her waist. She wore a plain green dress, with a grey shawl over her shoulders and several long necklaces hung around her neck. The main difference to her sister, though, was her eyes. They weren't cheerful like Noni's. They seemed sadder, somehow, and her manner seemed a bit on the cranky side – EVEN crankier than Noni.

'I see you haven't improved at the bagpipes, anyway,' said Noni. 'My ears are still ringing.'

'Well, some of us didn't get music lessons growing up, unlike other people I know,' said Noleen sharply. 'Anyway, my bagpipe-playing has other benefits. It keeps the rats and mice away from my pantry and it's very useful against intruders, as you have seen. Now, are you going to tell me why you're here for the first time in fifteen years, or are you just going to sit there eating all my beetle stew?'

Emma and Seán looked at each other in disgust

and slowly put their spoons down on the table.

Noni watched her sister scowling from the other end of the table and began to regret her decision to come to her house. There was, however, too much at stake, so she decided to grit her teeth and fill her sister in.

'There is a major problem in town.'

'Go on,' said Noeleen.

'Have you ever heard of the **Chawklit Spring?** The place where all the country's chawklit comes from?'

'I am aware of legends about that sort of thing, yes.'

'Well, it's not a legend. It's under Thomond Park stadium and it's very real.'

'There are fairies down there and everything!' said Seán excitedly.

'How wonderful,' said Noeleen, with no change in her expression.

'Well, not really,' continued Noni. 'The chawklit has been contaminated, poisoned even, and, if we don't find a way to fix it, it's going to put me and the fairies out of business. PERMANENTLY.'

Noeleen remained unmoved. 'That's a fascinating story, dear sister, but I fail to see what any of this has to do with me. I'm far beyond caring what happens to your precious pram business.'

Noni bit her tongue and did her best to continue the conversation. 'Magic.'

'What?' replied Noeleen.

'Gerry from the council believes the chawklit has been contaminated by magic; old magic that you might know about.'

Noeleen scoffed. 'Gerry from the council? Is that old codger still pretending to serve the city? The only thing he has ever served is himself. To a second helping of dessert. And what does he think *I* can do about any of this?'

Seán chimed in now. 'He thinks … well, *we think* that you might know a way to reverse the magic that has poisoned the chocolate and, you know, put it back the way it was.'

Noeleen looked at Seán's excited face and slowly turned her gaze to Noni.

'Well, well, well. After years of condemning, crit-icising and judging me for my interest in magic, suddenly you need my help to sort your little choco-late problem? Or should I say, "chawklit"? Ha! What are you like putting on that ridiculous posh accent? You always thought you were better than the rest of us, Noni. And now, after fifteen years, you come sneaking into my house with your two snotty-nosed accomplices looking for help with the very thing that caused you all to turn your backs on me!'

Noni leapt to her feet so fast she knocked her chair backwards on to the floor, startling Emma and Seán.

'I never had a problem with your magic,' she said sternly, as she pointed her long finger at Noleen. 'I had a problem with how you *used* that magic. And I had a problem with …' Noni stopped. She was begin-ning to get upset now. Seán and Emma had never seen her this way and were uncertain of how to react.

Noni gathered herself. 'I had a problem with what you did,' she hissed.

The children looked at each other, utterly confused.

'I knew we should never have come here,' continued Noni, beginning to move towards the door. 'C'mon, children. Let's get out of here. I can't be in the same room as this WITCH!'

'Actually, I see myself more as a spiritual herbalist but, you know, whatever,' said Noeleen with a smirk.

'Hold it right there!' shouted Seán who was now standing equidistant between the two women. Emma was taken aback by her little brother's outburst. 'Now, I know you two aren't the best of friends. I know you've had your problems.' His voice was quivering slightly. 'But people could *die* if we don't get that chocolate fountain back to normal. Do you understand?'

Noni, standing in the doorway, was shocked by her young helper's newfound confidence.

'He's right, you know,' said Emma. 'We need your help, Mrs Ogarty. You're the only one who knows enough about magic to find out what's going on. We need to work together.'

Noeleen pondered for a moment. She seemed impressed with the children's rousing speeches. She looked at them for a few seconds, her long hair hang-ing either side of her face like curtains.

'I might have misjudged you little urchins. You have character. Maybe you could teach that one a thing or two,' she said, throwing a glance at Noni, who frowned. 'Answer me this, though. Why would I help all those people in town who turned their backs on me, just like my family did? Why would I lift a finger to help them or the fairies or anyone else for that matter?'

'Because this is your chance to redeem yourself after what you did to our brother,' said Noni.

The cottage fell very silent except for the quiet crackling of the fire.

Noni walked back over to the table and placed her hands on its top. Fixing her gaze on Noeleen, she spoke slowly and clearly. 'You turned our brother into a raven.'

'What?!' gasped Emma. 'You mean … Francis is—'

'Our dear brother, Rita,' said Noni.

Noeleen looked uncomfortable. The children were in shock.

Noni continued, 'When our poor father died, he left his few paltry belongings to Rita, his only son. But Noeleen here felt that this was unfair, so she used her dark magic to turn him into a raven.'

'I had no choice! I had as much right to those things as he did!' argued Noeleen.

'OF COURSE YOU HAD A CHOICE!' shouted Noni. 'It was only a satchel, a few clothes and an old rock, for God's sake. The things Dad had with him when he drowned. Why did you even care that much? You did something unforgivable, Noeleen. Our poor brother is condemned to live the rest of his life as a raven, all over a few old rags. And I've had to look out for him all these years.'

The two sisters faced each other down. Noeleen stood with a defiant look on her face but soon that began to soften and she flopped down into the chair and put her head in her hands. She let out a deep sigh. After a pause she began to speak.

'I'm sorry. Really, I'm sorry, okay?' She looked up at Noni. 'I was so angry. I loved our father. I didn't see why Rita should get those things. I wanted them to remember him by. And I lost my temper and … it just … happened.'

'Can't you just turn him back to a boy? Surely it's not too late?' asked Seán.

'She can't because she doesn't even know how she did it in the first place,' said Noni, shaking her head in disgust. 'Some witch.'

Seán was confused.

'But why is Francis called Francis and not Rita? That *is* his name.'

'Because,' answered Noni, 'even though his big sister had done this terrible thing to him, he still didn't want her to get into trouble. So, he asked us to change his name and tell everyone that he had left town for work.'

Noeleen sat in silence staring at the floor. A tear ran down her cheek.

Emma moved closer to Noeleen. 'This is your chance to start to make up for things. If you can help us find out what's wrong with the chocolate you could really do something good.'

'You could save lives,' said Seán.

'Instead of ruining them, like you ruined Rita's,' said Noni.

After some time, Noeleen spoke. 'Even if I *did* want to help you, I'd need some of that poisoned chocolate, and I'm not leaving here. I haven't stepped foot in the city in over a decade.'

'No need,' said Noni, 'I have some of it right here.' She reached into her coat pockets and pulled out some of the sticky mess.

'And, thanks to Noni, I also have some in my hood,' said a not-too-pleased Emma.

Noeleen weighed up her options. She wiped her eyes. 'Fine, I'll look into it but I'm not promising anything, and I'm doing this for Rita, not you and your silly chocolate business, Noni.'

Noni rolled her eyes. Noeleen moved over to her table that was covered with strange objects and jars. 'Bring it here.' After rooting around in some tiny drawers, she produced a small bowl and scraped some of the sludge into it. She then opened a bronze-coloured tin and sprinkled a pinch of some of the powdery contents on top of the sludge.

'Stand back,' she said, as she lit a match and threw it at the bowl. A great ball of purplish light **EXPLODED** from the sludge and lit up the cottage momentarily. The blast was strong enough to knock a photo off the wall. Her cat, who had now realised he was not going to get any more snoozes today, leapt for cover and ran straight out of the front door. An acrid smell filled the air. They all coughed and Seán picked up the picture frame, which had broken when it fell.

'That's magic alright,' Noeleen said sternly. 'And no ordinary kind either. That's dark, forbidden magic. That hasn't been practised in these parts in hundreds of years. Not since the time of the High Kings of Ireland. Ye have your work cut out for ye here.'

'Who's this, Noeleen?' Seán asked, and handed the broken picture to her. It was a faded shot of a couple on their wedding day. A woman was smiling happily at her new husband as they stood outside a church and people threw confetti over them.

'That's Noeleen and **Mr Ogarty** on their wedding day, Seán,' said Noni tentatively. 'He's … not with us anymore.'

'What happened to him?'

Emma elbowed Seán and rolled her eyes at his tactlessness.

'Well, he ate the wrong kind of mushroom and died laughing. He laughed for two weeks until finally—'

'ENOUGH!' said Noeleen. 'You're always quick to talk about other people's business, Noni,' she snapped, as she gathered herself and shoved the picture to the back of a drawer. 'Do you want my help or not? I have things to be doing. Maybe you'd like to hear another song on the bagpipes?'

'NO, NO!' cried all three of them.

'Fine, then I'd better show you what you're dealing with.'

Noeleen lifted down a large book from a shelf. It seemed to take all her strength just to carry it to the table. She brushed away the dust and undid the large decorative metal clasp that held it shut. The pages inside were covered with ornate drawings and the writing was swirly and precise. Seán looked at the strange words on the yellowing pages.

'Wait, that looks like the fairy language from the stadium,' he said.

'The fairy culture stretches back thousands of years. Like them, the people who wrote this book had their own language and traditions,' said Noeleen. 'They were from another place and time.'

'You mean Caherdavin?' asked Noni. 'I can never understand what they're saying.'

'No, not Caherdavin, Noni. That's a mile from your house. This book was written by the wise ones who lived in these woods over a thousand years ago. They spoke the tongue of the **Tuatha Dé Danann,** a supernatural race of Celtic heroes, and were connected to all the **hidden dimensions.**' She looked down at the book. On one of the pages was a drawing of a man holding something bright blue in his hands, his arms raised above his head. Great shafts of light shone from the blue object and streaked out in all directions.

'Who's that?' asked Emma.

'That is **King Dagda.** He was a High King who was much loved by his people. He used the ancient magic to improve the land and help everyone who worked on it.'

'What's he holding?' asked Seán, eagerly sticking his face into the pages to get a better look.

'That is a **SKY CRYSTAL.** They were exceptionally powerful crystals capable of performing immense tasks. King Dagda used one to clean the rivers and lakes, grow bumper crops and even create protective shields around his lands.'

'That doesn't sound like bad magic to me,' said Emma. 'Why did they stop people from practising it?'

'Dagda was a good king but his son, **Eoghan?** Not so much. When his father died, he took the crystal and began to use it for nefarious purposes. That's the thing with a Sky Crystal. You can use it for good or evil. It depends on who's using it. Instead of helping his people, Eoghan used the Sky Crystal to hurt his enemies. He poisoned crops, contaminated water supplies and spread disease through neighbouring armies. He even used it to take control of the GREAT SOURCE.'

'What's the Great Source?' asked Emma.

Noeleen turned the page to reveal a picture of a large fortress surrounded by clouds. 'It's the original source of all the country's chocolate. It's where it begins its journey. Your **Chocolate Spring** is where the underground rivers and streams of chocolate eventually come out. To control the Spring, you have to protect the Great Source. That's why Eoghan built a castle over the very spot where the purest chocolate rises high in the mountains.'

'God, he sounds like no craic at all,' said Noni. 'He deserves a dead arm.'

'He got worse than that. Eventually, his dark magic became uncontrollable and the disease he had created with the crystal soon spread to his own lands and his own people. The darkness he unleashed turned everyone against each other, even the animals. One day, while high on his castle battlements, he was attacked by his own dog and fell to his DEATH.'

'What happened to his crystal?' asked Emma.

'It was decided that after all the hardship it had created, and to avoid it falling into the wrong hands again, it should be taken out to sea in a boat and thrown to the bottom of the ocean. It was never seen again.'

Emma and Seán were transfixed by the faded ancient drawings and Noeleen's hushed tone.

'Whoever is behind this is not to be trifled with,' she went on. 'To interfere in such powerful magic is incredibly dangerous.'

'Right so, let's forget it, then,' said Noni. 'C'mon, kids, let's go, I've a wash on and they're talking to a man who makes wooden ducks on the telly this afternoon. I can't miss it.' Noni headed for the door.

'Noni, wait!' said Emma. 'I don't like this any more than you do, but we have to find out who is poisoning the city's chocolate – we promised!'

Seán chimed in, 'And if you don't have any chocolate to sell, then we don't get to come over to your house anymore and help you make fake sweets.'

Noeleen was disgusted. 'Fake sweets? I can't believe you're still making them after … that INCIDENT! I can still feel the shame of it!'

'That was your own fault for stealing my merchandise, Noeleen,' said Noni, 'nothing to do with me.'

'Stop it, you two. Stay focused,' said Emma firmly.

She reached in and turned over the page of the ancient book to reveal a closer illustration of the large blue crystal. 'So, whoever is using this magic has to have one of these, right? A Sky Crystal?'

Noeleen nodded. 'Perhaps. It acts as a powerful energy amplifier, especially of negative energy. When used with dark intent, it can change the molecular structure and energetic frequency of anything it is focused on.'

'Like a pool of pure chocolate,' said Seán, suddenly understanding.

'I guess so,' said Noeleen.

'So, it's also possible,' added Emma excitedly, 'that if we find whoever has the crystal, we could use it to *reverse* the negative effects of the magic?'

'It's possible. But, like I said, that kind of magic hasn't been seen in hundreds of years. And whoever is behind this definitely doesn't want to be discovered.'

Emma was thinking a mile a minute.

'If they're poisoning the chocolate supply, then it can't be happening under Thomond Park.'

''Cos the fairies are guarding it all the time,' said Seán enthusiastically.

'Right,' said Emma.

'So where in the name of Holy St CJ Stander are they doing it then?' asked Noni, perplexed.

Noeleen flipped the page and tapped the spot with her finger.

'Right HERE.'

'Under your kitchen table?' asked Noni.

'No! Here on the map, YOU CLOWN! The site of the Great Source. The top of **Mount Mountain.**'

'Mount Mountain?' scoffed Noni. 'What kind of terrible name for a mountain is that? That's lazy mountain naming, if you ask me. It's like calling a town "Streetville".'

Seán laughed. 'Or a farmer "Mr Farmer"!' He and Emma chuckled.

'Look,' said Noeleen, gritting her teeth, 'I didn't make it up. Some ancestor did and I'm sure they had good reason. All I'm saying is that if you want to find whoever is behind this, you have to go here, to where the chocolate source rises.'

'To **King Eoghan's Castle!**' said Seán, who was loving the mystery of the whole tale.

'Well, what are we waiting for?' asked Emma. 'Let's go!'

'Hold on there one second, girlie,' said Noeleen. 'I admire your bravery, but that journey is fraught with danger. There are many trails to the top of Mount Mountain ...'

Noni sniggered at the name again, and Noeleen glared at her.

'But only one of them leads to the top safely.'

'How will we know which one to take?' asked Seán.

'I'll draw you a map.'

'Great!' said Seán.

'On one condition,' said Noeleen, as she eyeballed them. 'You never come back here and bother me again.'

The children nodded in agreement. Between the booby traps, the bagpipes and the beetle stew, they were very happy to oblige.

Noeleen sketched out the route for them on a scrappy bit of paper, then handed it to Seán. He tucked

it in his pocket, then looked
over towards the chute
they had arrived down.

'Erm, how do we …?'

'Follow me,' said
Noeleen, as she led Noni and
the children out of the front door and into a small
square courtyard. It was surrounded by a high bank
of earth on all sides. They could see now how far
down they had slid through the mushroom tunnel.
The house was completely built into the earthen wall
and the courtyard sat at the bottom of a deep hollow.
All around the walls were small doorways, and the
remnants of parts of old machinery lay scattered about
the place.

'Mind you don't fall over those things. They
belonged to my husband.' Unlocking one wooden
door, Noeleen revealed a spiral staircase inside.

'Up here,' she said, as they climbed skywards, before
pushing open a wicker flap at the top. They emerged
once more into the field beside the giant mushroom.

'What an … interesting place to live, Mrs Ogarty,' said Emma.

'I don't like visitors much,' she replied.

'You'd never guess,' said Noni sarcastically.

'I just feel sorry for your postman,' said Seán. 'How does he ever find your house?'

'I haven't seen him in a while, alright,' said Noeleen. 'Not that I'm complaining, he never shut up talking about the Mayo football team.'

Noni and the children looked at each other, all thinking of the skeleton in the booby trap.

'I wouldn't be expecting any parcels this week,' said Noni.

'Is it going to be another fifteen years, Noni?' asked Noeleen, as she folded her arms across her chest.

'I don't know, Noeleen,' said Noni solemnly. 'I can't forgive you for what you did to Rita. But you did something good here today so … who knows?'

'How is he? Rita … or Francis, I mean.'

'Come and meet him. He's waiting for us in the woods.'

Noeleen chewed her lip nervously. 'I can't … maybe next time.'

'Maybe next time,' agreed Noni, and she turned to join the children as they headed for the line of trees once again.

Noeleen stood by the giant mushroom as they disappeared into the woods. She shook her head slowly as she watched them go.

CHAPTER 6

With the map tucked safely away inside Noni's headscarf, she, Seán and Emma weren't long reaching Francis and the pram.

'Francis! Francis!' cried the children as they ran towards him. He had his headphones on and was cawing along to some positive affirmations on his audiobook. He was so in the zone he was oblivious to their arrival until they began to pet him.

'Some guard-bird you are. We could be chawk-lit thieves, for all you know!' barked Noni.

Emma placed her finger gently under Francis' beak and lifted his gaze to hers. She looked at him with kindness in her eyes.

'We heard what happened to you, Francis. What your sister did. We're so sorry you had to go through all that. Is that why you listen to all those self-help books and podcasts? To help you deal with the trauma of it all?' Francis let out a sad **SQUAWK.** He shuffled awkwardly from side to side on the handle of the pram.

'We heard you changed your name to protect her,' said Seán. 'You're a good man ... bird. And I read in a book that ravens can mimic human voices and sounds. They're one of the cleverest birds there is. But I guess you don't need us to tell you that,' he said, pointing to Francis' headphones.

'He sure is special, children,' said Noni, lifting Francis from his perch and putting him onto her shoulder. 'But he is the *WORST* security guard. Aren't you, kid?' Francis squawked a laugh and began to bob his head up and down, a sure sign that he was cheering up. 'I'll always mind you, little brother,' said Noni reassuringly, as she pushed the pram into the next part of their adventure, 'even if you do keep pooing on my good carpet.'

Back at the stadium, Chunks McSturdy and his team-mates were emerging from the dressing room and making their way to the team coach. Clearly in high spirits, they were celebrating another win.

'Great try, Chunks!' said an eager reporter, who walked hurriedly alongside him.

'Which one? I scored seven!' chuckled Chunks. Cameras flashed as photographers snapped a few more shots of the star player.

'How about a picture for the front of *The Times*, Chunks?' said one photographer.

'Sure thing,' said Chunks, 'always a fan of *The Daily Times* newspaper.' The camera clicked with a flash.

'Actually, it's *Gardening Times* magazine,' said the photographer sheepishly, 'I'm just a big fan.'

'Haha!' laughed Chunks. 'Well, my mam loves your magazine, so I guess it's okay.'

As he was about to step on to the team coach, Chunks caught a glimpse of the car park through the large gate. He could see Marguerite Shannon by her pram having words with three strange-looking men. They were big but oddly shaped and seemed to be hobbling about. Just then, a van pulled up and the men helped Marguerite and her pram into the back, then drove off. Chunks stood there, feeling unsettled.

'You coming, McSturdy?' yelled one of the players from inside the bus. 'Or are you waiting around for more adoring fans?'

Another player chimed in with a high-pitched impression. *'Ooh, Chunks, do your muscles need a massage after that tough game?'*

The big guffaw of laughter that followed from the rowdy team shifted Chunks' attention back to them and he climbed the coach steps. After one quick glance back towards where Marguerite had been, he joined in with the singing and jostling and the coach drove off.

Noni, Emma and Seán were now on a stony path that meandered through the trees. Noni pushed her pram up the incline, **HUFFING** and **PUFFING**, Francis perched in his usual spot on the handle.

'Are you okay with all this walking, Noni?' asked Seán, concerned.

'Not a bother, kid!' replied Noni confidently.

'Don't you get tired at … your age?' asked Emma tentatively.

'No, not since I had my hips replaced.'

'Did that help?' inquired Emma.

'Oh, it helped a lot. In fact, they did such a good job with my legs, I had hips put into my arms as well.'

The children looked at her, confused. 'What?'

'Oh, yeah,' said Noni matter-of-factly, 'they work like a charm. Although, it does throw up some issues from time to time. One time I went to shake the mayor's hand but instead I accidentally kicked him in the face.'

Francis squawked with laughter.

Just then they rounded a corner and came to an abrupt stop.

'Looks like this is the end of the road,' said Noni, 'but I don't see no mountain.'

The road turned into loose rock and rubble, then ended at a sheer rock face. They peered up, looking for a way over it, but it was far too high to climb. The wall of rock spread far into the trees on either side and any hope of going around it was blocked by impenetrable brambles and prickly gorse. The only thing to do was to go back the way they'd just come.

'Map, please, Noni,' said Emma, putting her hand out to Noni.

'Roger that,' said Noni, reaching deep into the recesses of her headscarf. She seemed to be taking a long time to locate it, but eventually she whipped out a piece of paper and handed it to Emma.

Emma looked at it more closely.

'Noni, this is a TV LICENCE.'

'Oh, is that where that went?' said Noni surprised. 'The fella came to the door and threatened to put me in jail 'cos I couldn't find it. Here!' She pulled another document from her headscarf.

'Noni, this is a takeaway menu from The Chicken Hut.'

'Saturday is Free Gravy Night, lads! If we leave now, we can beat the queues!'

Francis jumped up and down on the handle of the pram and bobbed his head in excitement.

'We love a bit of extra gravy, don't we, Francis?' said Noni, doing a giddy little dance.

'We can have gravy later, Noni. First we have the small matter of saving the country from poisoned chocolate?' said a frustrated Emma.

'Fine, ya gravy killjoy.'

After another lengthy search in her headgear, Noni finally produced Noeleen's map and Emma laid it out flat on the pram cover. She ran her finger along the trail they were meant to follow.

'We're here,' she said, 'and the road is supposed to keep going. But there's a cliff in our way.' The gang were perplexed.

'Maybe Noeleen was drunk,' suggested Noni. 'She was always tippling away at her weird home-brew concoctions. I once saw her drink fermented turnips and jump off the escalator in Penneys.'

'I knew this seemed crazy,' said Seán, as he sat down on a boulder, deflated. 'If Mount Mountain is so big, how come we've never seen it? It'd be hard to miss a giant mountain towering over the city.'

'Cheer up, kid. It wouldn't be the first time that my sister let someone down. Here, have a bonbon.'

Noni handed him a sweet from her pocket.

Seán sighed and popped the sweet in his mouth.

'Thanks, Noni. It's just … I was really hoping we could make a difference … that *I* could make a difference. To show people that I'm not just a "science nerd" and that …' He stopped talking and his face began to turn red. He looked at Noni with terror in his eyes.

'Noni … what kind of sweet is this?'

'Oh, Seán, I'm so sorry!' said Noni. 'I meant to give you a sweet from my other pocket. That was a prototype I've been working on. That's a "special bonbon" made from dog food and lemon toilet cleaner.'

'SPLEEUUUHH!' With all his might Seán suddenly spat the sweet out as hard as he could. The bonbon flew from his mouth and shot straight at Francis.

Francis shrieked with fright, leapt from the handle of the pram to avoid the missile, and flew in a flurry straight into the wall.

'Francis watch out for the w—' cried Emma, then stopped suddenly.

Francis had disappeared.

Seán dropped to his knees and began desperately scraping his tongue with his fingers. 'It tastes so bad! Like … dog … toilets!'

'Wait!' shouted Emma. 'Where's Francis?'

'What? What about me?' asked Seán, perplexed.

'He flew straight at that wall and disappeared! Noni, give me another bonbon!'

Noni hesitated. 'Okay, but if you suddenly lose your sight in one eye, it has nothing to do with me.'

'I'm not going to *eat* it, Noni! Just hand it over!' said Emma firmly.

'Fine so, but it's a waste of a good bonbon if you ask me.' Noni handed her the sweet from her pocket and Emma immediately flung it at the wall. It never landed. It simply went into the wall and never came back.

'What is happening? What's going on with that wall?' asked Seán, jumping to his feet.

'This could be some of that magic Noeleen told us about! She said King Dagda used the Sky Crystal to create protective shields around his lands. Maybe this is a special barrier to hide the Great Source. To keep people out!'

Seán and Emma moved towards the rock, but Noni was still unsure.

'How do we know what's on the other side?' she said nervously. 'It could be a dark, scary place with untold dangers and weirdos who suck your blood. Or worse, it could be Co. Clare!'

'Noni, Francis is in there, we need to find him,' said Seán.

'Do we, though?' asked Noni. 'He's always listening to those damn podcasts, and he's not a great security guard. He let that homeless fella have three Creme Eggs the other day. For free!'

'Noni! What happened to "I'll always mind you, little brother?" Francis is family and he's been through enough! **LET'S GO!'** said Emma defiantly.

Noni reluctantly agreed and, mumbling unintelligibly, moved her pram towards the wall.

'Okay, on the count of three,' said Emma, grabbing her brother with one hand and Noni's pram with the other. 'One … two …'

'I need to go to the toilet,' blurted out Noni. 'I drank two litres of undiluted Mi Wadi back there and I'm—'

Too late. Emma dragged them through the wall. There was a deafeningly loud **WHOOSHING** sound, spirals of colour everywhere and an incredible sense of falling – but not down. It seemed like they were falling *up,* and at terrific speed.

THEN EVERYTHING WENT DARK.

The three of them came to lying on their backs on rough ground.

'Where are we?' groaned Seán groggily, as he began to pick himself up. 'What just happened?'

'My chawklit! My chawklit!' cried Noni in a panic. 'Where's my chawklit? I can't see it. I can't see anything! I'm blind!' She rolled around on the path, flailing her arms and legs about.

'Noni, it's okay, your headscarf has fallen over your eyes!'

Seán bent to fix it and Noni began to calm down as she saw her pram was still intact.

'I'll be checking my inventory and if there's so much as a jelly baby missing from that pram, I'll sue the manager of this kip!'

'CAW! CAW!' they heard from a tree branch above. A little round beaked head looked down at them.

'Francis!' yelled Noni delightedly. 'You're here! We found you! They wanted to leave you here, but I insisted we look for you, kid.'

'What?' Seán couldn't believe what he was hearing.

'Guys!' gasped Emma. 'LOOK!'

The rough road they were standing on led straight to the foothills of a vast mountain which loomed large on the horizon ahead of them. Its base was covered in a dense forest of pine and spruce trees, but higher up its slopes was a hard coating of coarse rock and shale, the sky a deep blue behind it. It was an impressive sight.

'It's Mount Mountain!' said Seán excitedly. 'It's really there.'

'That protective shield has stopped anyone from really seeing it before. Maybe for hundreds of years,' said Emma. 'And up there is where we should find the chocolate source and whoever is tampering with it. And hopefully a Sky Crystal that can put everything right.' She pointed to the peak, barely visible beneath low cloud. Even with the cloud cover, however, it was just possible to make out the shape of some kind of structure at the top.

Just then, Francis squawked and landed on the handle of the pram. He had something in his beak.

'Whatcha got, Francis?' asked Seán, as he gently took the item from the raven's beak. Francis squawked loudly again. It was a piece of pink denim material.

Noni was horrified. 'There's only one person I know who wears bright pink in these parts. **Marguerite Shannon!**' Her eyes narrowed and her lips became a thin line. 'I *knew* she'd be part of this. She's probably up there laughing at us right now! She's poisoning the chawklit 'cos she knows that I always sell more than she does. She's always been jealous but this time she's taken it too far!'

Noni was getting very red in the face.

'Noni, this could have come from anyone,' Emma said. 'Don't you think you might be jumping to conclusions?'

Francis squawked again. They turned to look at him and he had something else in his mouth. It was a pink …

'Scrunchy! A PINK SCRUNCHY! And who do you think is trendy enough to wear such a garment in her greasy hair that's dyed off her head? I'll give you a clue. It starts with M and ends with DIRTY TRICKS!'

'You've got to admit it looks suspicious, sis,' said Seán. 'And from what Noni's told us about her, poisoning the chocolate sounds like something Marguerite would do.'

But Noni wasn't hanging around to debate the issue. She had already begun to head for Mount Mountain, fuelled by hatred for her archnemesis. The children looked on, bemused.

'She sure moves fast for an old lady,' said Seán, as he and Emma followed on behind.

They had soon reached the lower part of the mountain but Noni's pram began to struggle as they started to climb the rough ground.

'I'm not sure the suspension can take much more of this,' Noni said, as she pushed it over the loose rocks on the mountain path. 'This is the 1964 Babysafe XR TS7, not the TS8. She just wasn't built for it.'

'Why don't you leave the pram down at the bottom? We can collect it on the way back,' Seán said.

Noni stopped abruptly, horrified at the thought. 'What? Leave it at the bottom? On its own? Where anyone could find it and steal it? Would you ask Captain America to leave his shield behind? Or tell Thor not to bring his hammer? No chance! It's a part of him. And this pram is a part of me. It's an explosion of my body!'

'Don't you mean an *extension* of your body?' said Emma.

'Whatever! It's staying with me and that's that,' said Noni defiantly, and she continued to make her way over the rocks and stones with her chocolate cargo bouncing about inside the pram.

Before long, the way began to narrow, and Noni and the children found themselves on a winding mountain pass. On one side were tall spruce trees and on the other was a considerable drop down to rocks below. As the pram wheels ran along the bumpy path's edge, stones and debris dropped off the side and cascaded down the sheer face.

'Keep your wits about you, children, and watch where you're stepping. I'd like to give you back to your parents in as few pieces as possible,' warned Noni.

The children moved closer to the tree line and Emma questioned Noni as they walked.

'Noni, don't you think you've held on to these feelings towards Marguerite for long enough? I mean, the incident with your boyfriend was decades ago. Maybe she's changed over the years. Doesn't it take an awful lot of energy to hate someone that much for so long?'

'Hate is such a harsh word,' said Noni. 'I prefer … DESPISE.'

'Isn't that worse?' asked Emma.

'Look, you don't know how hard it's been for me over the years. I've had to work for everything I've got. This pram, she didn't come cheap. I had to sell four million golf ball chung-gums to get this.' Noni also had a very particular way of saying 'chewing gum'.

'Weren't those golf ball chewing gums just marbles covered in bird poo?'

'It's true they were a little bit firmer than your average chung-gum, but they were *verrry* nutritious. Sure, those birds eat all kinds of healthy berries and things. And, after my father drowned, we all had to work really hard to help my mother put table on the food.'

'Don't you mean food on the table?'

'No, my mother was very superstitious. You know the way some people think it's bad luck to put shoes on the table? Well, she thought it was bad luck to put *anything* on the table. So, she put the food on the floor and then the table on top 'cos she didn't want to seem, you know, weird.'

Seán laughed. 'She sounds cool.'

'We all had jobs around Limerick City from a young age,' continued Noni. 'Five of my seventeen sisters worked in a fresh air factory on the Ennis Road.'

'What's a fresh air factory?' asked Seán.

'It's where they make fresh air, you clown. It doesn't grow on trees, you know. Another sister was in charge of making escalators go up instead of down. Two others worked for the county council as ghosts. The three eldest wrestled coyotes in the circus, the next one was a cleaner in the Museum of Uncomfortable Chairs. My brother, Rita, painted traffic lights.'

'He painted them?' said Emma.

'Oh, yeah. Before traffic lights were electric, every time they changed a man had to run over and paint them, from green to red and then back to green again.'

'Traffic must have taken ages,' said Seán.

'It did, but it was worse if you wanted to cross the road. The green man wasn't electric either. Every time you wanted to cross, my brother had to pour a tin of green paint over himself and shout, **"BEEP, BEEP, BEEP!"**'

'That leaves four sisters,' said Seán. 'What did they do?' It was hard to believe he was actually able to follow this bizarre family history.

'One became a nun with the Holy Sisters of the Slightly Worn-down Pencils and three others tragically died of wind poisoning.'

'Oh no,' said Emma, shocked.

'Yes, it was very sad. They came around a corner in the shopping centre and walked into an infected breeze. A week later, their whole bodies became wind and they blew out of a window in the hospital. Every time I feel a draught I wonder if it's Bernadette ...' said Noni wistfully.

'And Noeleen makes seventeen,' said Seán, proud of himself for actually keeping count.

Something had been niggling away at Emma since Noeleen's house.

'Noni, what was that "incident" Noeleen blamed you for back there?'

'Oh, that,' said Noni, shaking her head. 'That's when things got REALLY MESSY. Literally. You see, Noeleen didn't always live hidden away in those woods. She used to be the total opposite – a real townie. She went to every rugby game, went to every party and hung around with all the famous players from the team.'

'Those people in the pictures on her wall,' realised Emma.

'Exactly. She got so popular, they eventually voted her in as chairperson of the whole Munster club. It was the most exciting thing to happen to anyone in our family. Except for my other sister Sheila, who was voted "Most Likely to Fall Down a Flight of Stairs" in 1982.'

'Go on,' said Emma, fearing another Noni-style-tangent.

'Well, one night, Noeleen was giving a big presentation to celebrate the team winning the championship. But on the way into the stadium, she saw my pram outside and, because she thought she was *so* important, she decided to help herself to some of my sweets while my back was turned. Turns out, she accidentally grabbed a handful of "special" ones.'

'Uh-oh, been there,' said Seán knowingly.

'What happened?' asked Emma.

'Well, sometimes, as you know, my SWEETS are an acquired taste and can have differing effects on the body. Everyone's constitution is unique, and it really depends on your own particular digestive situation and—'

'Noni, what happened?' demanded Emma.

'She had the worst case of public diarrhoea I've ever witnessed,' said Noni, blessing herself.

'Oh, NO!' said Emma.

'Oh yes. Right in the middle of her big speech. People were so horrified, they had to cancel the night. Three guests left in an ambulance suffering from shock. People were screaming. Noeleen ran out of there as quick as she could, which wasn't easy because of … you know … the mess. After that night, because of the shame, she never set foot in town again.'

'And she blames you for that?' asked Emma.

'Yes!' replied Noni indignantly. 'Even though she's the one who stole from my pram. It's not my fault she took the wrong sweets and put on a bottom-fireworks display that Limerick will never forget.'

'I don't think we'll forget that story any time soon either ...' said Seán, looking slightly green around the gills.

'Yes, let's change the smelly subject,' said Noni cheerfully. 'Did I ever tell you about my plan to combine a Double Decker with a Flake? I call it the Double Fec—' She was cut off by a terrifying noise.

'*Raaaaaaaaaarrrrrrrrggggggghhhhnnn-nfffllllbbbbssstttrrruuunnnnttthhh!*'

'Holy Saint Fortnite of the Cranked-Up Scope Shot! What was *that*?' screamed Noni. The sound seemed to be coming from the trees further down the path.

'There's something in the woods – and it doesn't seem happy!' said Seán, trembling.

They could hear a menacing sound of **SNAPPING** sticks and **CRUNCHING** rocks coming from within the trees and, from the swaying of the treetops and the **BREAKING** of trunks, whatever was approaching was of a size not to be trifled with ...

CHAPTER 7

They all instinctively jumped behind Noni's pram. Not that it was going to offer a huge amount of protection. You don't tend to look at many action movies and see the hero diving for cover behind a 1960s pram. Even if it *is* a Babysafe XR TS7 with an easy store-away foldable system.

'I can't look!' said a terrified Emma, as she buried her head in her hands.

'I can't see anything!' said Seán, as whatever was coming towards them threw a cloud of dust and debris up into the air.

'I should be celebrating Chunks McSturdy scoring tries right now,' said Noni. 'This is **no craic!**'

A great dark shadow filled the width of the trail ahead as a creature emerged from the cover of trees.

'Raaaaaarrrrgggghhhnnnnppplllltttsssstth-hhrrrnnntttthh!' it roared, as it began to move slowly towards the cowering bunch. Francis did his best to frighten the thing away by flying above the pram flapping his wings, but a mid-sized raven can only do so much.

As the true horror of what was facing her and the children became apparent, Noni shrank even further behind the pram.

'That is one ugly yoke,' she said quietly, as they slowly peered around the pram to get a better look.

This was A BEAST LIKE NOTHING THEY HAD EVER SEEN BEFORE, not even in a story book. It had the rough shape of a human, as in it appeared to have legs, arms and a head, but that was where the similarity ended. It was as tall as a double-decker bus and coated in a kind of metallic substance, like dirty multi-coloured tinfoil all over

its entire body. It also seemed to be leaking a large amount of **OOZE** from beneath the metal coating, which dripped down onto the ground in big, disgusting dollops. It had hands but they were lumpy and undefined, like they had melted into misshapen claws. It did seem to have most of the usual facial components but nothing was in quite the right place. Its eyes were more like DARK, SEEPING HOLES and one was halfway down its face. Nostrils were not in short supply, as there were at least five of them, and they **BLASTED OUT SLIME** from seemingly random parts of the head. Its HUGE, gaping mouth hung open to reveal only a small number of teeth but, because of the sheer scale of the beast, each one was the size of a fridge. Saliva dripped from the creature's mouth in LONG, **disgusting strands** as it marched towards them.

'My God,' said Noni, 'I haven't seen anyone drool like that since they changed the gravy recipe at The Chicken Hut last summer. You see, they added more spice but still kept the texture and—'

'Noni!' screamed Emma, 'enough about the gravy! What are we going to do?'

But Seán already had a plan. 'Throw things at it!' He began to grab sweets from Noni's pram and fling them at the monster, which was now only about twenty feet away. 'C'mon! HELP ME!'

'My chawklit! What are you doing to my precious cargo? That's all coming out of your wages!' screamed Noni in horror.

'Stop being ridiculous and help!' shouted Emma, who now began to grab fistfuls of chocolate bars and hurl them at the creature's head. This didn't, unfortunately, have the desired effect. In fact, it seemed to be making the thing even more angry. As a Bounty bar flew through the air, the monster caught it in its lumpy hand and held the chocolate up to one of its eyes. After examining it for a few seconds it let out a pained and deafening roar and mangled the bar in its hand, flinging it to the ground. It eyeballed Noni and the kids and let out another roar in their direction.

'RAAAAARRRRTTTTTNNNNGGGRR-RROOOOTTHHHAAALLLSSSTTTHH!'

Dollops of drool hit the ground.

'What'll we do?' roared Seán, 'we're running out of ammo!' The pram stock was nearly empty.

'THE SPECIAL STASH!' yelled Emma, and she opened the secret compartment.

'What good will that do? He didn't flinch at the other ones!' shouted Seán.

'Noni's "special" sweets put eight people in hospital last year, it's worth a shot!' said Emma, picking up the chickpea Maltesers and hurling them at the monster. They flew past his head.

'Give me a go,' said Seán. He took aim and launched a handful of the nail varnish Skittles. They went straight into the beast's mouth.

'Great shot!' shouted Noni. 'You hit him straight in the gob!'

The dodgy missiles seemed to catch at the back of the creature's throat and he spluttered. Then his demeanour changed. He seemed to calm for a moment.

'Do it again, Seán, it's working!' shouted Emma.

This time Seán picked up a can of 6UP and BANG – right in the cakehole! The monster crunched the can and jets of fizzy drink shot out in all directions, including down its neck. It shook its head and roared angrily.

'That stuff is making him angry again. Throw these!' Emma handed Seán a pack of Noni's 'Choc-Balls' – brussels sprouts dipped in shed protector.

Seán took aim once more and, just as the creature took a breath to roar, it got a mouthful of Choc-Balls from Seán. It swallowed them whole and, again, seemed to calm, its expression changing. Well, as much as you can decipher expressions on a monster that has very vague eyes and way too many nostrils. But it definitely seemed to be less angry.

'It's the healthy ones!' cried Emma, suddenly realising what was happening. 'Well, the ones with vegetables inside. Throw them! I think he likes them!'

'Well, that is certainly a first. I hope he leaves a good review on Google,' said Noni, who was frantically trying to keep the children stocked with ammo. Francis began grabbing the treats with his beak and dive-bombing them at the monster's head.

Seán threw another few chickpea ones at the beast, then some peas covered in nail varnish, then some sprouts. Even if they didn't land in his mouth, the creature picked them up and started to eat them. When it realised Noni's illegal treats were all gone, though, it started to get worked up again.

'Gimme more, he's getting restless!' said Seán, ready to throw another veggie salvo.

'There aren't any left!' said Emma, desperately searching the pram.

The monster shook its head and pounded its chest, sending brown ooze spurting out in all directions. Then it let out an almighty roar and started to move towards them again.

Noni and the children stumbled backwards, doing everything they could to avoid the edge of the path and the sheer drop below. Francis flapped above their heads and attempted to dive-bomb the creature, but it swatted him away like a fly, knocking his headphones clean off his head in the process. As the monster reached the pram, it picked it up and, turning it upside down, shook it violently.

'MY PRAM!' roared Noni. 'Look what it's doing to my pram!'

Francis screeched and flapped his wings frantically.

Seán looked on, feeling helpless in the face of this terrifying monster who was waving Noni's prize possession around like a broken toy. He thought of the bigger kids in school who pushed him around and how he was sick and tired of feeling under attack. Suddenly, his expression changed. He took a deep breath and rose to his feet. He walked slowly and purposefully forward and stood right in front of the beast. It towered over him, drooling and snarling.

'Seán! What are you doing, you mad young fella?' cried Noni. 'C'mon, let's run for it!'

'I'm not running away anymore,' said Seán defiantly, even though his hands were shaking and his heart was nearly beating out of his chest. 'Put down that pram right now, you BIG … SLIMY … **BULLY!**'

Just then, Emma jumped to her feet and faced the monster down as well.

'You leave my little brother alone! He may be younger and very annoying and talk about the surface temperature of weird moons way too much, but we're a team! And if you have a problem with him, then you'd better go through me first!'

'And me!' said Noni, stepping up to stand beside the children. Francis landed on her shoulder and puffed out his feathery chest. Turning to the children, Noni spoke in a lower voice. 'I really don't know what your problem with running away is. It's really a great option in these scenarios. I can't recommend it enough.' Francis squawked in agreement.

The monster continued to shake the pram, ignoring the gang's defiant stand, and when it realised that there were no more 'treats' to be had inside, it let out a huge roar and flung the pram straight at Seán.

In an instant, Emma leapt into the air and pushed Seán out of the way of the falling pram. They both crashed into Noni, who fell backwards onto the ground and rolled over the edge of the path, Francis flapping up into the air in a panic. As Seán hit the dirt he just managed to grab Noni before she fell off the edge entirely. He had her by the coattails, as she dangled precariously over the high drop down to the jagged rocks below. Emma was desperately holding on to Seán to stop him sliding over the edge after Noni, but she was losing her grip.

'**AAAAH!**' cried Noni, looking down at the ground below. 'Help! I'm too young to die!' She looked back up at Seán. 'No smart comments, you.'

'Hang on!' screamed Emma, but she was straining under the combined weight of Seán and Noni and was beginning to be pulled slowly across the dust and gravel towards the edge. She was losing her grip on Seán's leg.

'Don't let go, Emma!' cried Seán. He looked back at the beast, who was now kicking the broken frame of the pram about in a rage and stamping on it.

'**I … CAN'T … HOLD … ON!**' gasped Emma. Pebbles fell from the ledge and flew past Noni's

head as she squeezed her eyes shut from fear.

'Your parents are going to kill me,' she whimpered. 'They said no crazy stuff.'

The monster stopped kicking the pram and looked over at the three of them struggling on the cliff's edge. It let out an angry roar and began to lumber slowly towards them.

'IT'S COMING FOR US!' cried Seán.

Seán's leg slipped out of Emma's hand some more. Francis flew down and tried to hold on to Seán's shirt with his beak, even though he was way too little to make any real difference. Just as Emma was about to let go altogether, another hand grabbed Seán and reefed him upwards, pulling Noni and the children onto the path and back to safety.

The three bedraggled heroes looked up in shock to see the figure of the homeless man from the stadium standing in front of them.

'Quick, give it these!' he said, emptying a sack of carrots and parsnips onto the ground.

Emma, Seán and Noni quickly grabbed handfuls of

the veg that had fallen from the sack and tossed them towards the beast, as Francis circled overhead. The creature let out a yelp and began to devour a bunch of carrots.

'It's working!' cried Seán. They fired as many as they could grab at the beast as he continued to devour every single vegetable. As the last carrot went into the creature's mouth, it sat back onto the ground with a **THUD** and let out a satisfied groan.

Noni and the children were exhausted. 'Is it … over?' asked Emma, panting.

'That'll keep it satisfied for a while, alright,' the man said with a smile.

'You! You're the one who has been hounding me for years for free chawklit!' said Noni accusingly.

'And I thank you from the bottom of my heart for all the kindness you have shown me over those years. Well, that these special children have, anyway.'

It was indeed the homeless man Seán and Emma had sneaked treats to every match day since they'd started working with Noni two years before. But he seemed different now, more confident somehow. And he wasn't dressed in the rags he could usually be seen in near the stadium. Tall and thin with grey hair slicked behind his ears, he was actually quite handsome for a man getting on in years. His jaw was square and a bright smile lit up his face. He wore a green jacket with lots of pockets on the front. In each pocket could be seen the tip of some kind of tool, like pliers, screwdrivers, measuring tapes and pencils.

The children were so relieved to see him, they jumped up and hugged him.

'Thank you,' said Seán, still breathing heavily, 'you saved our lives. What's your name?'

'I'm Tom. And don't worry. He won't harm you. Not now he's got his fill of the good stuff.'

'What … is he?' stammered Emma, dusting herself off.

'That, my young friends, is a **Creamachocamus.**'

'A creama-what?' said Noni.

'A Creama-choca-mus. Like hippopotamus but with more chocolate. It's a creature formed from discarded sweets. And, as you have learned, it is very dangerous when provoked.'

'Provoked?' said Noni, disgusted, 'He came running at us like Paul O'Connell with a toothache. We did nothing!'

'He thought it was feeding time, you see, and was upset when he realised you didn't have the healthy snacks he was looking for.' Tom looked around at the debris field in front of him. 'Judging by the amount of sweets on the ground, I can see you tried to feed him … a more relaxed diet.'

'What do you mean, he's made of old sweets?' asked Seán, still very confused.

Tom explained. 'You see that brown and black ooze coming from our friend here?'

'Yeah,' said Noni, scrunching up her face. 'I can't see him getting a job in the new Nivea ad on the telly, the poor craythur.'

'That's because he is made up entirely of putrefied, unwanted chocolate. Coffee creams, to be precise. And his metal coating is all the shiny foil from the chocolate wrappers.'

'Chawklit?' Noni was amazed. 'I haven't seen

chawklit that gone-off since the Italia '90 Easter eggs I sold last week.' She touched Emma on the arm. 'Remind me to go to that funeral on Tuesday.' She blessed herself and shook her head solemnly.

'Why coffee creams?' asked Seán.

'The coffee cream is the chocolate people hate the most. It's constantly left at the bottom of the chocolate box and, more often than not, ends up in the bin.'

'Rightly so,' said Noni, 'coffee creams are rank.'

Tom continued. 'Of course, there are other kinds of chocolates in there too. All the ones that no longer feature in your favourite Christmas boxes. Apricot Delight, Peanut Cracknell, he's even made up of those horrible cheese-and-onion-flavour chocolate bars. People spit or throw them out but no one ever thinks about where it all goes from there. They just unceremoniously dump them and never give them another thought. But those chocs have got to end up somewhere.'

'How did they end up here, on Mount Mountain?' asked Emma.

'All chocolate comes from the one source. I'm guessing that's got something to do with why you've come to these parts, Noni. And, just as it comes from this one source, it naturally wants to return to it at the end of its lifecycle.'

'But what if we've eaten it?' asked Seán.

'Well, if you've eaten it, then it mixes with your energy and becomes part of you. But if it's never eaten, and most coffee creams aren't, then they find a way to make it here to Mount Mountain. In rainwater drains, picked up by birds and animals, they all make it here eventually.'

'How does that explain Bugs Bunny over there?' asked Noni, nodding towards the Creamachocamus, who was sitting very placidly now, chewing the remains of a carrot. Francis was also now a lot calmer. He was keeping the monster company, pecking at left-over bits of parsnip by its feet, with his headphones back in their rightful place playing his favourite self-help audiobooks into his feathery ears.

'Well, the chocolate and foil is far too filthy to return to the pure chocolate pool that rises in the mountains.

So, the forgotten chocolates do the only thing they can.'

'Join together,' said Emma, who was now feeling very sorry for the creature that had scared the living daylights out of them all just a short time before.

'That's right. They join together and protect the source from outsiders.'

'I like coffee creams,' said Seán reassuringly. 'I always eat them.'

Suddenly a GIANT GLOB of monster drool landed on his face, courtesy of the Creamachocamus.

'Looks like he heard you. You've got a fan!' said Tom, as Emma and Noni laughed at Seán's slimy discomfort.

'He could have just high-fived me,' said Seán, cleaning his face with his sleeve.

'That still doesn't explain why he likes vegetables so much,' said Emma.

'Chocolate, in its purest form, is natural. It's healthy. It doesn't need extra sugar. The Creamachocamus is made up of discarded chocolate that has been mixed with all kinds of additives. So, when he sees unhealthy bars and sweets, he gets upset, because he knows the way this is going to end. But Noni's veg-based treats seem to have tickled his palate. Which is surprising because they've damn near killed me a few times.' Tom directed his comments at Noni.

She looked sheepish. 'Well, you must have got me on a bad week,' she said, laughing nervously.

'Noni, look!' Seán was standing over the pram. Well, what was left of it after the monster had dropped it. It was in a very bad way.

'Sacred Heart of the Perpetual Justin Bieber!' cried Noni in anguish, as she dropped to her knees in front of it. **'MY PRECIOUS PRAM!** My beautiful 1964 Babysafe XR TS7 with quick release wheels and classic grip handle! It's banjaxed!'

She jumped to her feet and went for the Creama-chocamus, as Francis flapped around her head in an effort to offer protection.

Seán and Emma grabbed her and held her back. It wasn't easy to hold her, as Noni was surprisingly strong for a … whatever-year-old.

'Noni, he's not worth it!' exclaimed Emma.

Chapter 7

'I'll kick your coffee behind so hard you'll be pooing cappuccinos for a week!' yelled Noni, her arms flailing around.

Seán pleaded with her. 'It was just doing what it was created to do, Noni. It doesn't know any better.'

Noni struggled for a bit more but eventually her anger lessened, and she threw herself to the ground beside her pram, overcome with emotion.

'My poor pram. It's smashed to bits. It's more unfixable than my front door,' she sobbed.

'Don't worry, everybody. I'll have that thing back selling overpriced out-of-date treats in no time. Come with me,' said Tom, and he picked up the broken pram and flung it over his shoulder.

Emma watched him, finding it hard to believe that this was the same stooped guy who had limped and lurched his way around the grounds of Thomond Park all those times before.

'Who are you really?' she asked curiously. 'And how do you know about Mount Mountain and all the legends?'

'The name is Tom. **Tom Ogarty.**'

Noni and the children looked at each other, stunned. Mr Ogarty? Noleen's husband? Wasn't he supposed to be dead? Laughed to death? Even Francis was wide-beaked with surprise and lifted his headphones to hear more.

Tom was amused by their shocked expressions.

Noni broke the silence. 'Cripes, it is you! I didn't recognise you. What have you been using as moisturiser for the last fifteen years – gravel?'

'Looks like I have some explaining to do. Come on. I'll tell you all about it over some food. You're probably famished. Don't worry, I don't serve **coffee creams,**' he said cheerfully, as he led them off the path and into the woods.

CHAPTER 8

After a short walk, they entered a clearing and came upon an old mine. Entrances to the old shafts were mostly boarded up, except for one. Tom led them inside it, flicking a switch on the wall to light up the tunnel. Seán and Emma hesitated at the entrance, Noni a few steps behind.

'Don't worry,' said Tom, 'It's perfectly safe. Or would you rather take your chances out here with the big fella when he gets hungry again?' He made a persuasive argument, so they all pressed ahead.

Tom slid the rickety door back on a very ancient-looking elevator and he, Noni, the children, Francis and a very broken pram all squeezed inside like sardines. Sliding the door shut, Tom pressed a big green button on a transformer that hung on a cable. After a number of high-pitched squeaks and squealing metal sounds, the lift shuddered and began to move slowly downwards. Francis jumped on to Noni's shoulder for some extra security. Noni put her hand on his wing to reassure him.

'Don't worry, Francis, love, we're just disappearing down a black hole inside a deathtrap owned by a man who's being lying about his identity for years. Nothing to be concerned about.'

As they descended deeper into the mine, they caught glimpses of different levels where old mining machinery lay strewn about, each new floor briefly lit up by the solitary lightbulb hanging over their heads. The **judder** of the elevator echoed through the caverns as it continued **DOWN**

AND

DOWN.

'What *is* this place?' asked Emma uncomfortably, holding her brother's hand a little tighter than usual.

'These are **King Dagda's Mines**. Once a thriving underground wonder but now totally abandoned. Long ago, these shafts and tunnels were filled with the sounds of hundreds of workers, all hammering and chiselling away, but that's all gone now,' said Tom, his loud voice booming around the dark spaces.

'What happened to them all?' asked Seán.

'Dagda's son, Eoghan, used DARK MAGIC to poison the rivers and streams and contaminate the mines. And with the magic barrier in place, over time everyone forgot it even existed. Which suits me fine. I got the old place up and running and it's perfect for what I need. Peace and quiet and space to do my thing.'

There was a loud grinding sound and the lift shuddered to a halt.

'This is our stop,' said Tom. 'Mind your step alighting from the carriage,' he added in his best train-announcer voice.

Noni and the children couldn't see where they were stepping. There was barely any light to speak of beyond the elevator doors.

'What are you, a bat?' asked Noni, grumpily. 'I can't see my hand in front of my face!'

'One minute,' replied Tom, as he disappeared into the shadows. The gang heard the sound of some things being knocked over and rolling across the floor. 'Let's shed some light on the situation, shall we?'

Tom **SLAMMED** down a large handle embedded in the wall. There was a loud clunking sound and suddenly the whole room lit up as powerful ceiling lights came on one by one, spreading right back into the recesses of a large cavern. Seán and Emma rubbed their eyes as they slowly became accustomed to the light.

'COOL!' said Seán excitedly, as he moved quickly to explore his surroundings.

'Welcome to my humble abode,' said Tom, as he cleared some things out of their path. 'Mind your heads. It's not terribly tidy at the moment, I don't tend to get many visitors. In fact, you're my first ones. This calls for some tea!'

He moved to a small kitchen area and began preparing refreshments.

Emma and Noni crouched their heads to avoid the plethora of strange-looking tools and trinkets hanging from the rough cave roof. But as they moved through the chamber, it widened and the roof became much higher. Instead of the dusty, rough and rocky entrance way, they were now inside a large shiny metallic workshop filled with **weird** and **wonderful** contraptions and electronics. The walls were lined with what looked like control panels, which were blinking with different coloured lights and making low beeping sounds.

'What does that do?' asked a very excitable Seán, pointing, as he stared wide-eyed at a screen.

'It regulates the core mine temperature.'

'And that?'

'That controls my security cameras and alarms for the entire perimeter.'

'Cool. And that?' asked Seán, pointing to another screen.

'That's a microwave. It's where I heat my beans.'

'Cool …' said Seán, who was not really listening anymore, he was so lost in the wonder of it all.

Emma wandered about the main space looking at the contraptions in various stages of completion. One looked like a large umbrella but with solar panels on the top. Another looked like a great metal octopus but with rubber gloves on the end of its legs. In the middle of the room was a machine that looked like a big gun with a funnel attached to it. At the other end of the room was a badly charred shop mannequin filled with what looked like bullet holes. It had clearly been through the wars. Emma reached up to touch the machine.

'Eh, I wouldn't do that if I were you, Emma. That fires bullet gums. Not unless you'd like to inflict some unnecessary pain on your younger brother down there.' He nodded towards Seán, who had wandered over to take a look at the not-very-bulletproof dummy. Little coloured balls lay strewn around the floor. Emma gingerly took a step back from the gun. She looked around the room in awe.

'**WOW,**' she said, 'this is just like a—'

'A James Bond movie?' asked Tom.

'Yeah, that's what I was going to say. A James Bond film set!'

'Great! That's exactly the look I was going for.' Tom looked chuffed as he handed a cup of tea and a plate of biscuits to Noni, who had flopped down into a big leather armchair, not unlike one you would see a Bond villain in, menacingly caressing a cat.

'I designed this whole wall based on the first movie, *Dr. No*. That ceiling is inspired by the villain's one in *You Only Live Twice*.' They looked up at the beautiful smooth dome above them, its deep bronze colour stretching all the way up to a pendant light in the centre.

'So, you like the baddies then?' asked Emma nervously, beginning to question her decision to venture down here.

'God, no. Too much paperwork with all that scheming and plotting and over-throwing. My favourite character has always been Q.'

'I hate queues,' Noni chimed in from her armchair. 'You should see The Chicken Hut on a Saturday night after bingo. Out the door and around the corner!'

'He means the character Q, Noni,' said Seán, as he pinched a biscuit from Noni's plate. 'He's the quiet guy who makes all the inventions and spy gear for James Bond.'

'Yeah,' said Emma excitedly, 'pens that turn into guns. Shoes that shoot poison-darts.'

'A walking stick that's half-walking stick, half-GRENADE LAUNCHER!' shouted Seán with a grin.

'Sure, that's nothing,' said Noni, 'I once combined a Flake and a Double Decker to make a Double Fec—'

'What's that?' interrupted Seán. He was pointing to something over at the side of the room, which was covered in a large beige tarpaulin. He was surprised he hadn't noticed it before, because it was quite large, larger than anything else in the room. It was sitting in the half-light and had piqued his interest.

'Well,' said Tom, 'this is what you kids have been helping me with for the last few years.'

'Us?' said Emma and Seán together.

'That's right. Ladies and gentlemen –'

Francis, who was now perched on top of the funnel gun, let out a **SQUAWK.**

'My apologies. Ladies, gentlemen and distinguished ravens …'

Francis nodded his head in appreciation.

'May I present my latest invention.' He grabbed the cover and pulled it off dramatically. 'The **Candyrocopter-craft ... thing!** I really need to work on the name.'

The cover dropped to reveal a magnificent but utterly confusing contraption. It was a bit like a helicopter, but it also had short, stumpy wings. Instead of wheels, it had one ski and one giant claw. All over the body of the 'craft' were aerials and lights and, off the back, what looked like a ship's sail. The surface was a shiny silver and a glass dome sat over a space for two seats and not much else. Stunned silence filled the room.

'That's ... interesting,' said Emma, in the kindest tone she could muster.

'That's the ugliest thing I've seen since the Hulk's passport photo,' said Noni, appalled.

'Don't let the unique look put you off,' said Tom proudly, 'this baby PACKS A PUNCH! And *you* helped me build it.'

Emma chuckled. 'I think I'd remember if I'd built ... that.'

Tom put his hand on the side of the vessel. 'See this silver coating? That's made from the foil from all those treats you kids gave me.'

'Really?' gasped Seán.

'Yes, I required a very particular thinness of gold and silver foil which you can only get on chocolate bars. Better for solar power *and* aerodynamics. That's what I've used on the sail too. And watch this.' He opened a flap on the side and flicked a switch. The whole machine sprang into life. After a bit of a bone-shaking start, the vibrations lessened and it seemed to gently bounce on the spot. The sail **FLAPPED** on the back, aerials spun and lights flashed and **BEEPED.**

'Wanna see how the suspension operates on this bad boy?' Tom stretched down to a lower panel and flipped it open to reveal a complex system of moving parts, all hissing and adjusting in unison.

'Are they …?' Emma was shocked.

'Yes! Crisp packets! The very ones you sneaked to me while Noni wasn't looking.'

Noni scowled. 'They better not be the deluxe ones

that I robbed from the … I mean … that fell off that truck driving by that day …' She trailed off into an awkward mumble.

'What are they doing in there?' asked Seán, as he leant down to get a closer look.

'They're inflating, pressurising and releasing air. They act as a hydraulic suspension system that is suitable for all terrains and ensures a safe landing.'

'They're all cheese-and-onion flavour,' noted Emma.

'Yes, well spotted,' said Tom, 'I tried all the different flavour bags, but these were consistently the best. The **Salt and Vinegar** were too acidic and kept burning through the cables. **Smokey Bacon** caused too much smoke. And **Prawn Cocktail** … well, nobody likes **Prawn Cocktail**.'

Everyone, including Francis, nodded in agreement.

'Can we take it for a spin, Mr Ogarty? It looks like fun!' Seán was completely sold on the invention.

'I'm afraid that's not possible.'

'Go on,' said Noni. 'Let him have a go. He only gets sick on rollercoasters. And hurdy-gurdys. And speedboats. And bicycles. And skateboards. And foot-paths. And my carpet. Come to think of it, he gets sick on everything. I hope you know a good dry-cleaner.'

Seán gave her a look.

Tom continued. 'I can't give you a go because it won't fly.'

'What?' exclaimed Emma.

'Yep, that's why it has sat under this cover for months. Whatever I do, I can't seem to make it fly. I don't under-stand it. I've done all the computations. Right down to the type of bubblegum I'm using to secure the flaps.'

'Hubba Bubba,' Seán whispered to Emma.

'Definitely the best,' Emma agreed.

'But no matter what I do, I can't get her to lift off the ground. I really should have solved this problem by now.'

Just then, the microwave let out three long beeps. 'Ah! That'll be the beans! Grub's up, everyone.'

Tom led the gang to the table for some nourish-ment. Pushing some scrolls of blueprints and complex drawings onto the floor, he plonked three bowls of beans down in front of Noni and the children.

'Thanks! Did you know there are approximately 465 beans in every can of baked beans?' asked Seán proudly.

Tom chuckled. 'I can't believe that fact slipped by me.'

Francis let out an impatient **SQUAWK.**

'Don't worry my feathered friend, I haven't forgotten you,' said Tom, as he put a hollowed-out Creme Egg filled with beans in front of the raven. 'I suspect you're the kind of bird who enjoys fine dining, Francis.' Francis clapped his wings in approval.

'Isn't it time you explained how you're dead?' asked Emma, through a mouthful of beans.

'But not dead,' added Seán, between slurps.

'I suppose you're right,' said Tom, and he started to explain.

Over the years, Noeleen had become more and more obsessed with her magical potions and elixirs and less and less interested in her husband. She complained about his inventions getting in the way in the house so pushed them – and him – outside and into the dusty shed at the back. After weeks of uncomfortable nights, Tom decided it was time to leave. Noeleen decided to concoct a story that Tom was dead, rather than admit that he'd left her.

'Worse than that,' added Tom, as he sat down with his own bowl of food, 'she told everyone that I died from mushroom poisoning, laughing my head off. She didn't even give me a dignified death! Couldn't I have died saving an animal from the river, or being over-powered by a tornado or something? Mushrooms? Really?' He shook his head as he took a mouthful of beans.

'So how did you end up here?' asked Emma.

'Simple,' Tom replied. 'Money. Because Noeleen reported me dead, my life insurance paid out. I made her give it to me so I could build this place. After seeing all her old maps and books, I knew this would be a perfect, quiet location. But my ideas were bigger than my payout and I'd soon spent every penny of it. After that, well, I had to beg for food and cash to keep myself going.'

'Weren't you lonely?' asked Seán.

'Not at all. I had my inventions for company!' he said with a grin.

'And now us …' replied Emma nervously.

'Yes! And a great thing it is to finally be able to repay your kindness!'

'With a bowl of beans?' said Noni sarcastically. 'OH STOP, YOU'RE SPOILING US!'

'Not just beans,' said Tom. 'I'm gonna pimp your pram for you too!' He grabbed the battered shop on wheels excitedly and began to roll it deeper into his workshop. Francis flapped after it worriedly.

'Don't you worry, my feathered friend, I'll take good care of her!'

'You'd better!' shrieked Noni.

'It's okay, Noni,' called Tom, from the recesses of the underground chamber, 'she'll be better than ever when I've finished with her. Now, get some rest you lot, you've had a long journey. This will be ready when you wake up.'

There was no need to tell Seán and Emma to go to sleep. Their bellies full, they were leaning against each other on a comfy couch, already snoring.

Noni beckoned Francis over.

'C'mon, Francis, love, let's have a little nap. Just a short one, though. At my age, you're never sure whether you're actually going to wake up again ...'

Her loyal raven flew down and snuggled into her overcoat and they soon dozed off.

'**AaaaHOOOGaaaa!**' The sound of a loud horn woke Seán and Emma with a start. Francis jumped to attention also but Noni, still in the middle of a dream, continued talking loudly in her sleep.

'If you touch that Yorkie, you pay for it!' she screamed, clearly rowing with a customer somewhere in her subconscious.

Francis slapped her gently in the face with his wings. She soon came to and looked around, confused.

'Here you are, ready to go; meet **NONI'S PRAM – 2.0!**' said Tom proudly.

'**Wow!**' said Seán, jumping out of his chair. 'That is *sick*!' What used to be a battered brown pram with a gammy wheel and a droopy cover was now a bright red and orange dynamic super-pram. It had shiny alloy wheels, low suspension and a flame design right down the side.

'Check it out!' said Tom enthusiastically, as he flipped open a panel on the handle of the pram to reveal a row of switches.

He flicked the first one and the pram lifted up on its suspension with a powerful hiss. 'Off-road mode!' said Tom. 'For rougher terrain. Don't want that new body work damaged on rocky ground.'

'Press the next one!' shouted Seán in excitement.

Tom flicked the next button and a compartment drawer shot out the side.

'Oh my God,' said Noni, 'is that a …?'

'Yep, a proper secure secret compartment for your … ahem … SPECIAL treats.'

'I'd like to see Garda Ryan find that one!' said Noni, delighted.

'What's that button, Mr Ogarty?' asked Emma, pointing to a red one.

'Press it and see.'

Emma pressed the button and the pram immediately started up with the growl of a monster truck. They all jumped back in fright.

'What's happening?' shouted Seán, hands over his ears.

'You'll see,' said Tom, arms folded confidently in front of him. The pram began to widen and extend and the base rotated to reveal four seats. From the hood, a steering wheel emerged with a whirr and turned to face the seats. With a large **CLUNK,** everything settled into place and the revs in the motor dropped to a less deafening volume.

'WOW!' cried Seán, 'It's a … pram-car!'

'What do you think, Noni?' asked Tom. 'Pushing a pram is over-rated, wouldn't you say?'

Noni was speechless.

'It's the only three-litre 200 horsepower V8 pram in the whole county, I'd say. Probably in all the world.'

Noni touched the pram tentatively. She ran her bony fingers along the side, feeling its new smooth exterior.

'It's so red,' she said softly. 'Like my late father's eyes after the Limerick Races. Top speed?'

'Forty miles an hour. Double that going downhill,' replied Tom matter-of-factly.

'Gears?'

'Six.'

'Transmission?'

'Automatic.'

'Chill cabinet?'

'Of course.'

'Sound system?'

'Blaupunkt.'

'Tax?'

'Technically it's still a classic, so it's next to nothing.'

Noni still seemed a little stunned. 'This is the most impressive thing I've seen since Ben Shanahan's dog drove that jet ski through the pharmacy window. And he didn't even have a prescription.'

'What are we waiting for, Noni? LET'S GO! We've got a Sky Crystal to find,' said Emma, as she and Seán jumped in.

'Oh, I nearly forgot,' said Tom, as he reached into his pocket. 'Put this on.' He slid a candy bracelet on to Noni's wrist.

'Lord above, it's a long time since anyone gave me jewellery,' she said, blushing. 'The only bracelet I ever got was when I was in hospital for gallstones. But you're technically still married to my sister. This is highly inappropriate.'

'Relax, it's not jewellery. And it's not real candy. It's whistle-activated and is directly linked to your pram.

If you get into any danger, just put your lips together and blow.'

'But I can't—'

'**AaaaHOOOGaaaa!**' Seán had clearly found the horn.

'**Hop in, Noni!** I've even turned on the heated seat for you!'

Tom pulled a handle on the wall and a metal door slid upwards to reveal a ramp. Noni climbed in, Francis on her shoulder.

'Follow the ramp upwards. It'll take you to the rear of the mine and out onto the road to the summit. Are you sure you're okay driving it, Noni?'

Noni was getting used to the feel of the steering wheel in her hands. 'I think so. Although the last car I drove was steam-powered.'

'You'll soon get the hang of it. Just make sure you take a left at—' But he was cut off as Noni slammed her foot down hard on the accelerator and the pram shot off towards the exit.

'**Wooooooooooo-Hooooooooooo!**'

yelled Noni, as the g-force made her headscarf fly backwards.

'Bye, Mr Ogarty!' shouted Seán, as the new and improved pram roared through the doorway. 'And thanks for all the **beaaaaaannnnnssss!**'

Their voices disappeared into the depths of the mine.

Tom smiled and turned to clean up the dishes they'd left on the table. As he leaned across to pick up one of the bowls, the craziest thought entered his head ...

CHAPTER 9

The growling sounds of the pram's new engine echoed around the dark caverns as they drove at speed up the twisting and turning ramp. The beams from the headlights flashed around the walls and every now and again they caught a glimpse of a disused mine shaft or some other piece of abandoned equipment. Noni was taking to driving her pram like a footpath to chewing gum and was in her element. Maybe too much so. Bent over the steering wheel with a crazed look on her face, she was paying little or no attention to the route they were taking and, as they approached a fork in the tunnel, she kept to the right and pumped the gas. The wheels skidded in the loose dirt as she increased her speed, crunching over a fallen sign that read: **'DANGER!'**

As they rose through the underground levels, the ramp suddenly began to steepen and, as they accelerated upwards, pinned to their seats, it became clear that there was no obvious exit up ahead, just a dark passage that seemed to be blocked with debris. It also became clear that Noni had no plan to stop any time soon.

'Noni! SLOW DOWN!' screamed Emma, 'the road is blocked!'

'Relax your cacks,' said Noni coolly. 'I know what I'm doing. You might want to hold on to something.'

Francis grabbed on to Noni's head in terror, but, in doing so, he also put his wings across her eyes.

'AAAAHHHH!' cried Noni, 'Francis, I can't see!'

There was an almighty smash as the pram crashed through some wooden crates, shovels, old ropes and pulleys. There seemed to be no reduction in speed as Noni floored the pram, and buckets, pots and pans went flying through the air.

Seán and Emma had slid down into their seats and were cowering from the flying debris. In the commotion, it was hard to see where they were headed. Suddenly, there was daylight and the vehicle was being whacked by the leaves and branches of trees until, eventually, it shot through the foliage and landed with a **BANG** on a path.

Emma reached up and **YANKED** the steering wheel to the left, sending them into a spin. As the wheels spun on the dirt and they all yelled for their lives, the pram eventually came to a stop underneath a big oak tree.

The children slowly emerged from deep in their seats, relieved to find that they were more or less unharmed.

Noni, however, still had Francis' wings wrapped across her eyes and was continuing to scream at the top of her aged lungs.

'AAAAAAAAAHHHHHHHHHHHH!'

'Noni! It's okay, we've stopped! We're safe!' shouted Emma.

'AAAAAAAAAHHHHHHHHHHHH!'

Noni continued to scream.

Seán tried to get through to her. 'Noni, it's okay, we're out of danger!'

Still the screaming continued.

Emma had a thought. 'Noni, I know where you can get half-price chocolate!'

The screaming stopped instantly.

'Where is it and how much is there?' said Noni calmly, back to her official business tone.

The kids giggled and sighed with relief now that calm had been restored.

Francis flopped back into the backseat, emotionally drained, headphones dangling from his neck.

'Maybe I'd better drive ...' said Emma.

Despite the ordeal Noni had put it through since leaving the mine, the pram, apart from a few scrapes and scratches, was still in pretty good shape. A testament to Tom's craftsmanship, it had handled the rough terrain with ease and was now humming along as they traversed the mountain passes and elevated trails. Evening was setting in, the fields far below them now blanketed in a soft mist and the air becoming a little cooler as the friends continued on their trek.

Chapter 9

'Does any of this put you off the whole chocolate business, Noni?' asked Emma, as she drove confidently past spruce trees and rocky outcrops.

'God, no. And how often do I have to tell you? It's pronounced "chawwwwklit"!'

'Of course, sorry,' said Emma, glancing at Seán, who rolled his eyes.

'I can't imagine ever doing anything else,' said Noni. 'It's always been me and my pram, for as long as I can remember. Sure, what else could I do?'

'You could be a stunt driver,' said Seán, chuckling.

'You know, people will let you down. They come and go and promise you all kinds of things, but this pram? This pram is always there. It's part of me now and as long as I have strength in my bones and a good lawyer, I'll always sell my chawklit and sweets to anyone foolish … I mean, happy enough to buy them.' Francis let out a cheerful squawk from the back. 'What about you, children? What do *you* want to do when you grow up?'

'I'm going to be an astronaut,' said Seán confidently.

'Ooh, that sounds great. My uncle was an astronaut,' replied Noni.

'Really?'

'No, sorry, he delivered pizzas. I always get them mixed up. He had a helmet for the motorbike though. That's like an astronaut.'

'I'm going to be an **extreme-sports-expert-adventurer-explorer-businesswoman,**' chimed in Emma, who was sitting back with her arm resting on the side of the pram, like a woman used to the good life.

'Are you now?' asked Noni.

'When I'm finished winning skateboarding competitions, and Seán is back from space, we're gonna start our own **chocolate company.** And we're not going to have just one pram, we're going to have a whole fleet of them, selling chocolate all over the country. Every game in every town, our crew will be there.'

Seán thought this was hilarious.

'Yeah, and we'll be absolutely coining it. If you play your cards right, Noni, we might even hire you,' he said with a chuckle.

'Oh, really?' Noni raised an eyebrow at him.

'Yes, really,' said Seán, laughing, 'but you'd better pull your socks up.'

'Well, you cheeky pup, firstly, I don't wear socks. I wear tights. And secondly, I always wear three pairs and they're always pulled up. I could catch a chill in a house fire.'

'Well, how about you give us better pay and working conditions, then, Noni? And we'll remember that when we make our first million and buy you out,' said Emma, all business-like.

'Okay, I'll give you a ten per cent pay rise,' said Noni at last.

Emma laughed. 'Ten per cent of nothing is still nothing, Noni!'

'It's still ten per cent,' said Noni with a smirk, as the pram trundled on through the evening air under the watchful eye of Mount Mountain.

Emma brought the pram to a stop. It was at least two hours since they left Tom's place and her eyes were tired from focusing hard on navigating the narrow trail.

'We're here,' said Emma examining the landscape around her. After getting no response, she turned to the others only to find they had all fallen asleep again. 'Hey, WAKE UP, this is the end of the line.'

Francis rubbed his eyes with his feathers, his head-phones on as usual. Seán stretched and yawned but Noni was still out for the count. Her head was lolling over the back of the seat and she was drooling on to her shoulder.

Seán gave her a gentle shake. 'Noni, wake up.'

She sat up with a start. 'Your honour, I've never seen those jelly babies in my life!'

'It's okay, Noni, we're here. And I think something is happening up ahead.'

'Where's here?' asked Seán.

Noni gathered herself and tried to adjust to her new surroundings. Night was beginning to fall, and the pram was parked at the end of a trail. It was clear if they wanted to proceed any further, they would have to climb and scramble up through the rocks and gorse. There wasn't much daylight left and the moon was already bright in the sky.

'Noeleen's map. Have you still got it?' Seán asked Emma. 'Are we in the right place? Is this where the Sky Crystal is?'

'I stopped using that map ages ago,' said Emma. 'First it nearly got us killed by that … creature, and then it seemed to trail off into nowhere.'

'So how did you get us here without a map?'

'Easy. Pram sat nav! Mr Ogarty built it in.'

'That's all very well,' said Noni, looking worried, 'but either my stomach is grumbling like I've eaten hot wings, or something is happening over there.' The sound of what seemed like drumming was coming from beyond a ridge above them.

'We must be close to where the **Great Source** rises. C'mon,' said Emma, as she led the way up through the rocks, with Francis flapping closely behind them. As they reached the top they peered over to see where the sound was coming from.

Noni arrived last, clearly uncomfortable.

'I'm after ripping my favourite tights on a gorse bush. I got them for President Kennedy's visit to Ireland in 1963. They were second-hand but were still in good cond—'

She stopped in her tracks. 'What in the name of Saint Terry Wogan is happening down there?'

From their vantage point, they were looking down on a flat area that was lit up by flaming torches, placed around in a wide circle. All of this was happening within the crumbling walls of a ruin perched right on top of the mountain. Part of a tower still stood at one corner and contained the narrow slitted windows favoured by archers of the time. An archway entrance still remained mostly intact, its original wooden doorway long since decayed away. By its dimensions, this had once been a great building, but now only remnants of its thick walls remained, laid out at differing heights around the rocky summit.

'Eohgan's fortress!' said Seán in amazement. 'It must be. The ancient book was right. The Sky

Crystal must be close,' whispered Emma, her eyes glowing orange from the reflected flames.

In the centre of the fiery circle within the castle walls was a dark, steaming pool. The steam rose high into the air as the liquid **HISSED** and spat and bubbles burst. Although all of this was indeed very odd, stranger by far were the creatures that surrounded the pool. They were bigger than any men the children had ever seen, with huge, humped shoulders. Even from up on the ridge, Noni and the children could see their misshapen faces and strange lumpy ears. Each of them had a drum hanging from their neck and they were banging them in unison.

Boom, boom, boom. Boom, boom, boom. The slow rhythm continued as the figures **GRUNTED** and jerked around the edge of the pool of bubbling liquid.

'This is either some sort of magic ceremony or a really terrible disco,' whispered Noni.

'Well, then that must be the DJ,' said Seán, nodding towards the other side of the pool. A shadowy figure, dressed in a cloak, stood on a great stone altar, arms raised high in the air. The figure held something aloft and chanted aloud.

'I think we've found the Great Source. But this looks sinister,' said Emma, 'and there are a lot of them. Way more than I expected. We should go and get some help …'

As Emma turned around to face the others, she saw that five of the huge beasts were now towering over them. One of the beasts was pointing a tube directly at them.

'Too late, kid,' said Noni, as the beast sprayed a foul-smelling gas from the tube directly into their faces.

The thing about hanging upside down is that it's very disorientating.

When Emma, Seán, Noni and Francis woke up, they had no idea which way was up and which was down. Everything seemed to be mixed up. They were drowsy and confused, though they did still have a

sense that they were in great danger. But here's the thing. They were laughing. Like, laughing their heads off. It was the kind of laughter you can't help when you're with your best friend and they've just said something really funny and neither of you can stop the uncontrollable guffaws that are spilling out of you and you feel like if you don't stop laughing soon, then someone is going to be sick. Noni and the children, and even Francis, were laughing to the point of puking, but they also had absolutely no idea why. It was difficult to speak but Seán tried his best.

'Ha! ha! ha! ha! … what … ha! ha! ha! ha! … is … happening … ha! ha! ha! ha?!'

'Ha! ha! ha! I don't … ha! ha! … know … ha! ha! but I think … ha! ha! we're in … ha! ha! ha! terrific danger! Ha! ha! ha!' said Emma, through the howls of laughter.

'Ha! ha! ha!' said Noni, 'I … haven't … ha! ha! … laughed this much … ha! ha! ha! … since … ha! ha! ha! … black pudding was declared a superfood. Ha! ha! ha!'

'Ha! ha! ha! Whatever they sprayed us with must be some kind of … ha! ha! ha! laughing gas. Oh my God! Ha! ha! ha!' said Emma, 'Look … ha! ha! ha! … where … ha! ha! ha! … we are!'

As the gang made sense of their surroundings, it became clear that things were not ideal. They were in a net, on top of each other, dangling precariously over a TOXIC POOL OF SCALDING CHOCO-LATE. It was the same gunk from under the stadium, but this pool was larger and looked deeper and more ominous.

'Is that … ha! ha! ha!' laughed Seán.

'Yes … ha! ha! ha!' roared Emma, 'like the pool Gerry showed us … ha! ha! ha!'

'We're all … ha! ha! ha! going to die!' shrieked Noni.

'Ha! ha! ha! ha! ha! ha!' They were all in stitches, including Francis, who was squashed between Noni and Seán and squawking with uncontrollable laughter.

'I'm glad you all find this so amusing,' said a voice from nearby. Through the mesh of the net, they could just about make out a dark figure in robes standing on the large altar beside them. It was the same person they had seen from up on the ridge.

'It won't seem fun for long. I can guarantee you that.' The voice seemed familiar to Noni but with all the drumming and shouting in the background she couldn't quite make it out.

'Who are you? Ha! ha! ha!' asked Noni through the laughs. 'And what … ha! ha! ha! have you done with my pram?' There was no answer and the air continued to fill with smoke and the sound of drumming.

Emma held her breath to avoid the awful smell rising up from the pool and suddenly realised she was laughing less. She was soon down to just a giggle. 'Hold your breath, Seán!' she whispered.

'Ha! ha! ha! What?' said Seán.

'Hold your breath … ha! ha! It helps with the laughing. You too, Francis.'

They all began to hold their breath and soon the strong effects of the debilitating laughter lessened. Looking down at the molten mixture below them, the seriousness of their predicament became apparent.

'We need to get out of here,' said Emma, desperately tugging at the net that held them captive. The giant man-beasts were dancing and shouting just a few metres away and the firelight was illuminating their fearsome faces.

'They look like **ogres**,' said Emma, horrified.

Noni looked closer. 'They're no ogres. They're something far darker – retired rugby players!'

'Rugby players?'

'Oh, yes. Look at the way they're stooped and broken from playing game after game. Their ears no longer look like ears, just lumps of battered cartilage from endless scrums. I've seen the poor brutes hanging around the stadium after matches. It's like they have no purpose in life, forced to roam the land talking to anyone who will listen about matches they should have won decades before. But nobody cares …'

The robed figure became more animated as the rugby players banged their drums and moved in a circle around the opening of the Great Source. The leader began to chant, holding what was now visible as **a very large blue crystal** above their head. A shaft of moonlight cut through the steam and smoke, bounced off the crystal and shone directly into the bubbling sludge. It seemed to be making the toxic chocolate even more volatile.

'The Sky Crystal! That must be it!' cried Seán.

The beasts' chanting grew louder and as it did so, the crystal seemed to become brighter and brighter in the hands of the leader of this bizarre ceremony. Noni, Francis and the children looked on helplessly, dangling in their net above. As the bright blue light from the stone got stronger, Noni caught a glimpse of something on the altar. The feet of the shadowy robed figure were lit up momentarily to reveal – **a pair of pink wellies!**

'I *knew* it!' squealed Noni through the net, her eyes burning with anger. 'I knew she was behind this! Marguerite Shannon! You'll pay for this, **YOU DIRTY EEJIT!'**

With that, the chanting stopped and the owner of the pink wellies began to roar with laughter. Maniacal laughter, with all kinds of devilment rolled in.

'What are you laughing at, Marguerite?! You know that by destroying the chawklit source you'll not only ruin *my* career but yours too! You can't sell chawklit if it's poisoned!'

Finally, the figure stopped cackling and began to lower her hood.

'That's where you're wrong, Noni. I have no interest in selling old tat from a pram. That's the kind of thing my **cheap, ungrateful** sister would do.'

The hood fell to reveal none other than Noni's sister, Noeleen.

'WHAT?!' said Emma and Seán together.

CHAPTER 10

I n the name of Holy Limerick ham, what are you *doing*, Noeleen?'

Noeleen threw her head back in laughter. 'Isn't it obvious, Noni? I'm ruining the supply of chocolate to the entire city and I'm going to dispose of you and your meddling urchins in the process. Oh, yes, and our flea-ridden brother Rita as well.'

Noni and the children were stunned. Francis squawked with anger.

'I hope you enjoyed my special mushroom gas. It's

good to laugh. At least until I make you cry again.'

'Why are you doing this?' cried Emma. 'You said you were sorry about Francis! You were going to do something good!'

'Sorry about Francis? Ha! There was no way I was going to let him take my father's belongings. I needed them!' said Noeleen.

'Why do you still care so much about Daddy's old bag of rubbish, Noeleen?' cried Noni.

'That's what you're wrong about, dear sister. It was anything but a bag of rubbish. On the day our father drowned he had found something very special on the bed of the estuary. Something that had been lost for over a thousand years.'

Noni was shocked.

'You don't mean that old rock in his satchel was—'

'Top marks, Noni! A SKY CRYSTAL! Our father found the only surviving stone buried deep underwater. He gave his life for this stone, and I wasn't about to let Rita, you or anyone else take it away from me!'

'But you could have used that crystal for good, to help people, like King Dagda did!' shouted Emma over the noise of the drumming and the bubbling chocolate.

'I could, I suppose, but where's the fun in that? Besides, it has taken me years to finally work out how to harness its **true power.** And I am going to unleash that power on everyone who laughed at me that night of the ... INCIDENT!'

'You mean the diarrhoea?' asked Noni. 'I told you that had nothing to do with me, you took those sweet—'

'Silence!' shrieked Noeleen. 'Don't say that word!'

'What word?' replied Noni innocently. 'Diarrhoea?'

'Stop it!' roared Noeleen. 'I have been forced to live in exile since that night. While you, Noni, got to spend your life surrounded by the players, the fans, the club. They were my world, Noni! And you took them away from me. Now you'll never see the bright lights of the city again.'

'Bright lights of the city? Are we both talking about the same place? I don't think anywhere in Limerick stretches past a forty-watt bulb,' scoffed Noni.

'Laugh it up, sis. You have about five minutes before you get a demise fit for the most annoying confectionery seller this side of the Shannon. **Death by chocolate!**'

'It's pronounced chawklit!' said Noni defiantly.

'Thank you for making it so easy to get all of you up here by the way, Noni. For once, I'm glad you're always sticking your nose in where it isn't needed. Well, the last thing you'll stick your nose in is that pool of boiling goop. It'll do wonders for your complexion. You could do with some help at your age.'

'But wait,' said Seán. 'What about the pink wellies? Where did you get them?'

'Oh yes!' said Noeleen, rubbing her hands together with a delighted cackle. 'Thank you for reminding me! Oh, the shoes aren't mine. I just borrowed them. I don't get the chance to pop into town for decent foot-wear these days, you know.' She turned to her rugby henchmen and shouted, 'Bring her to me!'

They heard a van door slide open somewhere in the shadows and the silhouettes of some figures moved towards them. As they emerged into the light by the pool, Noni and the children gasped. A very dishevelled Marguerite Shannon was being led towards them by two of Noeleen's goons.

'Marguerite?' exclaimed Noni. 'What happened to you?'

'Turns out this Little Miss Busy-Body followed you and Gerry down to the fairies' workshop under the stadium,' said Noeleen. 'Then she tried to warn Chunks. We'll see how much they like to eat those fancy new **protein bars** of hers when they're more poisonous than a three-week-old snackbox! Ha! Ha! Ha!'

The rugby players scooped Marguerite up and, climbing onto the wooden platform the net was suspended from, they dropped her right in on top of Noni, Francis and the children.

'Ouch! Mind my head! I only have the one. It's getting a bit crowded in here,' said Noni, not too happy at being so close to her archenemy.

'Look, Noni,' said Marguerite, trying to adjust herself so Noni's knees weren't in her face. 'I'm not exactly ecstatic with this arrangement, either. I was just doing the same as you, trying to protect our chocolate and all the people who eat it. When I saw Gerry bringing you into the back of the stadium, I knew something was up. I had to warn Chunks.'

'Why, so you can steal another boyfriend from me, Marguerite?'

'For goodness' sake, Noni, that was years ago. And Chunks is not my boyfriend. We're business partners.'

Noni was still unconvinced.

'It all sounds very convenient, Marguerite. How do we know you're not in on this whole thing?'

'Well, Noni, I know you wear glasses but even *you* can see that I'm about to be turned into hot choco-late, just like you lot.'

Noni looked down at the bubbling pool beneath them. She had to admit, things were not looking good for any of them.

'ENOUGH YAPPIN', the sky is nearly right. Begin the final ritual!' yelled Noeleen.

'Let us go!' shouted Noni, 'You don't need to do this, Noeleen!'

'On the contrary, my dear sister, I do! For this spell to work, I need to give energy to get energy. And that's where you lot come in. You'll be my very chocolatey sacrifices to give the crystals balance.'

'SACRIFICES!' screamed Marguerite in terror. 'But I'm too young and good-looking to die!'

'Young? Who are you kidding, Marguerite? Just because you wear teenagers' clothes, that doesn't make you a teenager,' scoffed Noni.

'How dare you?' retorted Marguerite.

'Stop arguing!' pleaded Seán. 'How are we going to get out of here?'

Emma stared down at the rugby players as they began to bang their drums in unison. She was thinking hard but coming up with nothing.

The chants grew louder and more sinister as the misshapen players moved to the rhythm, marching in a circle around the chocolate pool as Noni, Marguerite, the kids and Francis hung helplessly above it in the net.

Noeleen held the Sky Crystal high above her head and began speaking in a loud, ancient-sounding language. She was shouting upwards at the sky, as if pleading with it to do something.

Suddenly, the moon emerged from behind a cloud and a shaft of light shot from it down onto her crystal. The crystal let out a high-pitched sound that made the gang in the net cover their ears. Noeleen struggled under the force of the beam, but her chanting became louder and her face almost seemed to distort as the exploding blue light now illuminated the whole mountaintop.

'Look at her eyes!' shouted Seán, as he poked his hand through the net. Noeleen's eyes were now the same colour as the light hitting the crystal. It was as if the light was filling her, as well as the crystal.

She began to speak, her voice now even deeper and more terrifying: 'Lower them,' she said to the beasts on the wooden platform. 'As the light grows to its strongest point, THEIR ENERGY WILL FEED MINE!'

The large figures of the rugby players, now almost completely engulfed by the growing blue light, began to unwind a pulley. The net jolted momentarily. Everyone inside it screamed.

'What are we going to do?' wailed Emma.

Francis tried to bite the rope with his beak in desperation.

'I'm sorry, kids. Maybe your parents were right, I *am* a bad influence!' Noni put her head in her hands.

But Noeleen seemed to be struggling under the power of her own crystal, and light began to shoot from her eyes and mouth. She laughed hysterically as the new power coursed through her body. The chocolate pool was fizzing and hissing, and it too glowed blue from the powerful magic.

The net made another jolt and the prisoners all screamed. Suddenly, there was a **PINGING** sound and two of the rugby players fell to the ground. Then more **PINGS** and two more fell. It wasn't obvious what had caused them to fall over until Seán spied some coloured balls rolling on the ground near the fallen beasts.

'Bullet gums!' he shouted.

Just then, they heard a thundering sound high above them. It sounded a bit like a helicopter.

Marguerite, who had covered her face with her hands, peered through her fingers into the sky to see where it was coming from. She was utterly confused by what she saw.

'What is that … thing?'

The others did their best to adjust themselves so that they could look.

Emma squealed. 'I don't believe it! It's Tom!'

'And he's in the Candyrocopter-craft … thing! He made it fly!' shouted Seán, delighted and relieved to see the contraption overhead. As cumbersome and strange as the craft was, it was doing a good job at hovering above them, despite the turbulence and wind being created by the powerful spell that had engulfed the mountaintop.

'Who's that with him?' shouted Emma. There was someone else on board and he appeared to be manning a large gun mounted on the front. It was the same gun that the kids had witnessed in Tom's lab.

'It looks like … It can't be!' said Emma, as she squinted into the sky. 'It looks like—'

'Chunks McSturdy!' said Noni and Marguerite in unison, then gave each other dirty looks for daring to utter their hero's name.

'Chunks! Down here, pet!' shouted Marguerite. Noni rolled her eyes.

'Shush!' shouted Emma, 'Tom is trying to say something!' It was hard to hear him above the noise of the Candyrocopter and the high-pitched sounds from the crystal. The craft was about a hundred feet in the air and Tom was signalling and yelling something at the gang below.

Noeleen was now also staring upwards and she did not look happy.

'Continue with the spell!' she shouted at her crew of beastly helpers. 'Drop them into the chocolate, we must do this now! Cut the rope!'

'No!' shouted Emma helplessly. One of the burly rugby players produced a knife and was about to slash the rope when he was suddenly struck in the head by a missile from above. He fell to the ground, unconscious, his knife sliding off the platform and dropping into the pool below.

Seán gave a loud cheer. Chunks waved at them from his perch on the big gun.

Tom was still shouting and signalling at them, this time pointing at his wrist.

'He wants to know the time,' said Noni. 'It's about ten o'clock!' she yelled upwards. 'The clocks go forward

next week so it'll be great for the long evenings!'

'No, Noni! He means *your* wrist. The bracelet! The one he gave you!'

'Oh yeah!' She pulled up her sleeve to reveal the bracelet, which was, thankfully, still on her wrist. 'What did he say to do again?'

'Whistle, Noni!' shouted Seán. 'YOU'VE GOT TO WHISTLE!'

Noni tried but all she managed was to spit all over Marguerite's face.

'Hey! Watch it! Say it, don't spray it!' said Marguerite in disgust.

'I can't whistle. I only got these teeth on eBay last week. Somebody else whistle for the love of God!' Everyone looked at each other with blank expressions.

'You mean to tell me not one of you can whistle? What are the chances of that?' said Noni, perplexed.

'Well, it's a common fact that 67 per cent of people cannot whistle and only 13 per cent of people say they can actually whistle well,' said Seán, delighted with an opportunity to show off his scientific knowledge.

'I think I preferred the facts about the donkeys,' said Noni regretfully.

By now, the rugby players had started to throw rocks up at the Candyrocopter, which was now ducking and diving through the air and firing all kinds of sweets at the mob below. Mints, toffees and bonbons all bounced and ricocheted off the rocks.

'Not the lemon ones! What a waste!' moaned Noni, shaking her head.

Noeleen continued her chanting as the pool became a bright fluorescent blue. 'Drop them in! Drop them in to the Great Source, damn it!' she commanded.

As the rugby players tried to make it to the platform holding Noni and the gang, Chunks sprayed them with high-velocity sweets from his gun. The beasts all dived for cover and yelped from the pain of the sweets hitting their target. Chunks laughed as they hit the deck – until suddenly his gun made a repetitive clicking sound. It was EMPTY.

Another rugby player ran across the wooden platform and tried to untie the rope holding the net.

Chunks saw what was happening and shouted to Tom, 'We're out of sweets and bullet gums, what else have you got?'

'Just these! Noni specials!' Tom passed Chunks a military-style weapons box. Chunks opened the lid and inside were all the weird chocolate knock-offs that Noni had given Tom over the years. 'Make 'em count! It's all we've got left!'

Chunks grabbed fistfuls of the dodgy chocolate bars and loaded them into the funnel of the gun. He slid back the loading mechanism and released it with a satisfying clunk. Swinging the gun to aim towards Noeleen below, he shouted at Tom, 'Bring me in close!'

Tom took a firmer grip of the joystick and the craft banked hard to the left and began a steep descent.

Noeleen held the crystal high above her head as its light beam continued to fill the pool. She shouted at the rugby player on the wooden platform, who was still trying desperately to untie the rope and release the prisoners into the pool.

'**FASTER, YOU IMBECILE!** This spell can't work until they're in that damn chocolate!'

The sound of the Candyrocopter turned to a shrill squeal as it dove downwards from the sky, Chunks ready at the gun.

'Hold! Hold!' said Tom, as he strained to keep control of his contraption. 'On my mark! Not until I say!'

Chunks looked down the barrel of his gun. He had the rugby player at the rope in his sights.

'I can take the shot!' he cried.

'Not yet!' shouted Tom, 'Just a little longer!'

As the rugby player below adjusted the rope, the net jolted once more and the gang screamed for their lives.

Tom reefed the joystick back towards him and the Candyrocopter strained as it tried to pull back up.

'Now!' he shouted.

'Twox away!' shouted Chunks as he squeezed the trigger and Twoxes, Nickers and Creepy Crawlies blasted from the gun. A Twox hit the rugby player square in the face and he was knocked clean off the platform.

'GOTCHA!' roared Chunks. Seán and Emma looked on and cheered. He swung the gun towards Noeleen.

'One more second!' he cried.

Tom was leaning right back, grabbing the throttle, as he tried to pull the craft into a climb. He could barely hold it. 'Take the shot!'

Chunks squeezed the trigger one more time. A Nickers bar shot out just as the craft banked upwards. It struck the Sky Crystal Noeleen was holding and there was a huge flash of light, followed by an enormous bang. The crystal blew apart in a multi-coloured explosion that leapt upwards into the sky.

Noni and the gang covered their faces as the light spread across the mountaintop.

The Candyrocopter tried to escape the blast but was caught in the shockwave as it climbed skyward. Chunks and Tom roared as they struggled to maintain control of the craft.

Suddenly everything went very dark and eerily quiet. The net swayed gently from side to side.

Noni lifted her face to look out.

'Is it over?'

'I … I think so,' said Emma. 'Tom and Chunks did it!'

'Eh, I wouldn't be twerking with delight just yet,' said Marguerite, looking upwards. The explosion had caused a fragment of the crystal to become embedded in the rope, which was now beginning to burn with a blue flame.

'Oh no! We need to get out of here! Noni, your bracelet, it could help us!' cried Emma desperately. 'Tom said to use it if you were in danger!'

'I think this qualifies as danger. I mean, we are about to die!' shouted Marguerite.

Noni kept trying to whistle but it just made her spit more. 'I knew I should have got these dentures in a medium!' she grumbled. 'They're too big for my mouth!'

The rope frayed and dropped the net lower. Now they were just a few feet away from becoming chocolate soup.

Just then the sound of a perfect whistle filled the air. Noni, Marguerite and the children looked at each other.

'Who was that?' asked Emma. Everyone shook their head. Then the whistle happened again. That's when they realised it wasn't coming from a human.

Francis, who was sitting on Noni's shoulder, let out another beautiful high-pitched whistle. He saw them looking and nodded, then put his headphones back on.

'There! The pram!' pointed Seán. 'When he whistles, Noni's bracelet calls the pram!' Over the ridge came Noni's new and improved pram, bouncing across the rough terrain. The rope continued to shred above their heads and with each **TWANG** it edged ever lower.

'Keep whistling, Francis!' cried Emma.

Francis whistled again and the pram continued at speed towards them, accelerated up a mound of rocks and grass and launched into the air. The gang's amazement was short-lived as the rope SNAPPED and they began to fall down towards the toxic pool. **'AAAHHHH!'** But instead of a splash, there was a **THUD.** They weren't covered in chocolate, they were in Noni's pram as it flew through the air, over the steaming chocolate pool and towards the ground on the far side. As it landed, it tipped sideways and dumped the gang out on to the earth in a heap.

'I'm blind!' shrieked Noni, clutching her headscarf, which had once again fallen over her eyes.

'It's okay, Noni, you're fine,' said Emma, as she lifted the scarf off Noni's face.

'Are we still alive?' asked Noni, breathless.

'I think so,' said Marguerite, 'but at your age, Noni, it's always touch and go, really.'

'At least I'm honest about my age!' said Noni sharply.

'Stop bickering, you two, and help us get out of this net,' said Emma, as they attempted to untangle themselves.

Seán was the first to get free. He dusted himself off and looked over at the pond.

'Shouldn't this be back to normal by now?' The chocolate was still angrily FIZZING and BUBBLING.

The others finally managed to escape the net.

'You always thought you were better than me, Noni!' came a distant voice.

All heads turned towards the great stone altar overlooking the pool. A very ragged and charred-looking Noeleen was struggling to stand on top of it. In each hand she held a chunk of broken Sky Crystal. 'Always the lucky one who got whatever she wanted. You're not going to get your way this time, though, Noni! This spell isn't over until I say it is!'

She held the two crystal pieces above her head and began chanting again. The crystals began to glow blue once more and the pool frothed and bubbled even more violently. 'You can't stop me, Noni! You can't st-**woooaahhh!**'

They looked on in amazement as Noeleen was suddenly lifted high into the sky. She had been grabbed by the claw of Tom's flying contraption and no amount of kicking her legs and flailing her arms would set her free.

As she waved her arms around, the two large crystal pieces fell down onto the ground, landing beside Seán and Emma. They picked them up. Despite Noeleen dropping the crystal pieces, the liquid chocolate was still **dark** and **putrid** and **frothing angrily**.

'What do we do? Noeleen's spell is still working,' said Seán, worried. 'The chocolate still looks contaminated.'

'Remember Noeleen's book,' said Emma. 'We have to use our good intentions.'

'Like King Dagda!' exclaimed Seán.

'Exactly!'

'But what can we do? We're just kids. How are

we going to match the magic of Noeleen? She's too powerful.'

Emma thought for a second. A flash of inspiration came across her face. 'Not if we all join together.' She took Seán's crystal piece and put it on the altar with hers. 'Now, everybody form a circle and hold hands.'

'Do we have to?' asked Noni, who was not at all keen on holding hands with Marguerite.

'Yeah, couldn't we just fist-bump instead?' pleaded Marguerite.

'Guys, c'mon! We have to give this a try,' said Seán, frustrated.

Noni, Marguerite, the children and Francis all held hands (and feathers) around the altar.

'Now what?' asked Noni.

'Everybody think positive, good intentions towards the chocolate and all the people who will eat it. Concentrate!' Emma closed her eyes tight. She opened them a few seconds later and saw the crystals were still dark. 'It's not working. Is everybody thinking pure and good intentions?'

Noni and Marguerite looked sheepish.

'I may have imagined Marguerite getting arrested by the police,' admitted Noni.

'And I may have imagined Noni's bum exploding,' added Marguerite.

'Good intentions!' yelled Seán and Emma together. The gang refocused their thoughts and suddenly the Sky Crystal pieces began to glow a **bright blue.** Seán opened his eyes and saw what was happening.

'It's working! Keep doing it!' Soon the blue light spread from the crystals and with a big *whoosh* filled the entire mountaintop. The power of the light blast rocked the Candyrocopter, and Noleen, who was still dangling from its claw, let out a shrill scream.

'Oh my God, look at our eyes!' cried Seán. The eyes of everyone in the circle, including Francis' little bird eyes, were shining bright blue as they struggled to hold on to each other in the turbulence being produced by the fiercely glowing Sky Crystal pieces. A powerful energy coursed through their bodies. Noni had an ecstatic look on her face.

'My God! I feel fifty years younger! I feel ... seventy-five!'

'How much longer, Emma?' cried Seán.

'I don't know!' she yelled above the wind and the swirling tornado of light that was now leaping and spiralling upward from the Great Source and filling the night sky above their heads. Suddenly, the light seemed to go into reverse and began moving from the sky back down into the chocolate pool at terrific speed. There was a **DEAFENING CLAP** and everyone in the circle was blown backwards onto the ground.

Everything became calm. The only sound was the hum of Tom and Chunks' craft still hovering above their heads.

Noni, Marguerite, Francis and the children slowly got to their feet, dazed from what had just happened.

'You did it!' yelled Tom from above. 'Look at the chocolate!' They all looked at the surface of the liquid in the opening of the chocolate source and saw that it had stopped bubbling and hissing and was now a warm, smooth and calm pool of delicious-looking and perfectly unmagically-contaminated chocolate.

'The Sky Crystal!' exclaimed Seán as he ran to the altar. The shards of broken crystal had been reduced to just two piles of fine dust. 'I guess no one else will be able to get their hands on it now. The chocolate is safe.'

A voice came from above.

'Put me down!' Noeleen screamed, as she hovered high over Noni and her friends. Her ex-husband laughed heartily.

'Who needs laughing mushrooms when you have something this funny to look at!'

Chunks was still perched on the Candyrocopter and chuckling merrily. 'You okay, folks?' he shouted down.

'We're great, pet! How are you, Chunks? You're looking great!' shouted Marguerite, while fixing her hair.

'*How are you, Chunks, you're looking great!*' said Noni sarcastically. 'You're something else, Marguerite Shannon. If you were a lollipop, you'd lick yourself.'

'You're just jealous, Noni, 'cos Chunks and me are sooo close.'

'Not as close as my boot will be to your backside, Marguerite, if you keep that up.' The two women's bickering was interrupted by the sound of some police jeeps skidding to a halt nearby and this time the only blue light was coming from their vehicles. Garda Ryan came over the ridge with Gerry Madden beside him.

'Is everyone okay?' said Gerry, as he made his way over. 'Chunks told me he was heading up here after he saw Marguerite being brought in this direction.'

He looked at Seán and Emma. 'I see you found Mount Mountain. Not a lot of people know about this place. I was on the force twenty years before I was told about it.'

'I don't think we'll be asking our parents to bring us here on holiday,' said Emma dryly.

'The fairies will be very grateful, Noni,' said Gerry, shaking her hand. 'They can't wait to get back to doing what they do best – **rotting people's teeth.**'

'Hey, if anyone is going to rot some teeth around

here, it's me,' replied Noni.

'And what am I,' remarked Marguerite indignantly, 'chopped liver?'

They were all distracted momentarily by Noeleen screaming abuse as the Candyrocopter lowered her down to the waiting police officers.

'What will happen to her?' asked Seán.

'I guess she'll have a long time to come up with some new magic spells where she's going, fella,' replied Garda Ryan. 'You did well here today, kids, but I think it's time you called it a night. Oh, and Noni?' he said, as he turned to walk back to his jeep.

'Yes, Garda Ryan?' said Noni, dripping in pure innocence.

'I'm still watching you …'

A long, loud whistle interrupted proceedings. The pram, which had been lying in its crashed position, suddenly flipped back onto its four wheels and the engine fired up again.

Francis let out a delighted squawk. He was very pleased with himself.

'Francis, where on earth did you learn to whistle?' asked Emma. The raven opened up one wing to reveal his audiobook player. He tapped on the screen with his beak so everyone could see the title: *Whistle Your Way to Happiness*. Everyone laughed.

'Sure, you're only a little legend!' cried Noni. 'For that, I'll let you off washing up tonight. Who fancies some dinner? Let's hope this Pram Nav knows where my house is ...'

As the pram took off back down the mountain, Seán piped up from the back. 'Noni? Do you mind if we make a small pitstop on the way back?'

Noni's pimped-up pram drove slowly down a road in a quiet housing estate. As they drove past the yellow streetlamps, Seán peered in at the houses.

'This is it,' he said with certainty. The pram stopped quietly outside one particular home. The lights were all off inside.

'Hit it, Noni.'

Noni leaned on the horn.

'**AAAAHOOOOOOOOGGAAAAA!**' went Tom's unique invention.

Within seconds, the front door opened and out walked Conor Delaney, the bully from the stadium. He was rubbing his eyes as if he'd been asleep. As he got nearer to the pram, his eyes widened in amazement.

'How'd you like the **bockety old pram** now?' said Seán proudly.

Conor stood looking at the shiny vehicle and was clearly impressed. He tried to hide his amazement, though, and barked back at Seán, 'I could still take it off you if I wanted to, **Science Boy.**'

Emma chuckled in disbelief. 'I don't know why you're calling him Science Boy. He's not the one wearing those space pyjamas!'

Looking down, Conor realised that he was out in

public wearing his favourite Mickey Mouse pyjamas, complete with patterns of rainbows, unicorns and Mickey Mouse dressed as an astronaut sitting on the back of a flying rocket.

'Space Mickey!' gasped Conor, as he quickly covered his body with his hands. Quick as a flash, he turned on his heels and ran back into the safety of his own house, slamming the door shut behind him.

'I guess I'm not the only science fan in school,' said Seán, beaming.

Noni, Emma, Seán and Francis could all still be heard laughing as their pram skidded out of the estate and off towards home.

'That was fantastic, Noni. I'd better not eat any more or I won't be allowed back on the team.' Chunks was rubbing his belly in satisfaction.

Tom agreed. 'Delicious, Noni. What was that gravy made of?'

'Chawklit,' replied Noni, as she cleared the plates.

'And the salad ... that was very unusual. What did you put in that?'

'Chawklit.'

'She puts it in everything, Tom. You get used to it,' said Emma with a sigh.

'Hey, Chunks,' she went on. 'I've been wondering. How did you know where we were? How did you end up in Mr Ogarty's Candyrocopter ... thing?'

Chunks handed his plate to Noni. She slipped it under the table. That plate was never going to be washed again. In fact, if she could only find a frame the right size she'd hang it up over the fireplace.

'I knew something wasn't right at the stadium,' said Chunks, interrupting Noni's thoughts. 'I didn't like the look of those guys I saw with Marguerite, so I got the bus to follow them.'

Marguerite rested her chin in her hands and looked across the table adoringly at Chunks.

'You're so thoughtful,' she said, misty-eyed. Noni rolled her eyes and stood up from the table.

Chunks continued. 'A couple of miles up the road,

I saw the van that she got into heading up a dirt track. I got off my team bus and decided to follow it. That's when I saw Tom flying around in his contraption. He said you guys had headed for the top of the mountain.'

'How did you get it to fly, Tom?' asked Seán, eagerly. 'What was the scientific breakthrough?'

'Simple,' replied Tom with a large grin on his face. **'Beans!'**

'What?' gasped Seán.

'After you left my workshop, I found myself staring at the empty bowls of beans. Then it hit me. If beans can cause such powerful explosions from … well, you know where, then it makes sense that they can act as a propulsion system for my craft. I made some quick adjustments to the engine to adapt it to bean power and hey presto! Up, up and away!'

'I think you'll have to call it a **Fartcopter** from now on, Tom!' said Chunks, laughing.

'Well, it *is* easier to say than Candyrocopter … thing!' said Tom chuckling.

'And finally!' said Noni loudly, as she walked back

to the table with a large, covered dish. Plonking it down in the middle of her guests, she picked up the hot lid with a tea-towel and dramatically lifted it off to reveal her culinary masterpiece. Everyone looked stunned.

'Noni's Beef Wellington!'

In the dish was a large crusty pie. And sticking out of the top was something very odd indeed.

Marguerite looked utterly horrified.

'Are those my … **good pink wellies?**' she said, as her jaw continued to drop lower. Sure enough, poking out from the thick pastry and, after a lengthy spell in Noni's oven, now melted almost beyond recognition, were Marguerite's signature pink wellington boots.

'They are indeed!' declared Noni triumphantly. 'Baked in thirteen different kinds of – you've guessed it – CHAWKLIT!'

'How dare you, **Noni Considine!**' shrieked Marguerite, leaping to her feet. 'I only took them off at your door to be polite! Those were designer wellies my father brought me back from Paris!'

'Designer *and* delicious!' said Noni with a devilish grin.

Marguerite went for Noni and the two began chasing each other around the table while everyone else looked on in hysterics.

Everyone, that is, except for Francis, who nestled down in his favourite spot in his favourite chair, shaking his head at the silliness of the two shrieking banshees. He took out his phone and hit play on the audiobook he was listening to, then popped on his headphones.

The title of the book appeared on the tiny screen:
'A Bird's-Eye View of Happiness.'

THE END

Acknowledgements

Thank you ...

To Dodo Reddan and all the wonderful characters of Limerick who inspired Noni.

To Corrina, Owen, Matthew, Rose and Buddy for encouraging me every day in trying new things.

To my best friend Marcus who kept the 'chawklit' memory alive for all those years.

To Dave, Maria, Eimear, Cathal, Alison, Róisín, Ziz, Ros, Peter, Phil, Simon, James and everyone at Today FM for their amazing support and for letting Noni leave two vintage prams permanently outside the studio.

To Sarah, Aoibheann, Teresa, Fiona, Paul, Linda and everyone at Gill Books for helping me dream this up.

To my wonderful editor Venetia for her patience and wisdom.

To my amazing team at NK Management – Niamh T, Niamh Mac, Niamh Kav, Andy and Noel – for your ongoing support and advice.

To Little Conor Murray, Little Keith Earls, CJ Stander and everyone at Munster Rugby for their laughs and support for Noni.

To Niall Breslin for his ongoing advice and support.

To everyone at Eason and all the amazing book-sellers around Ireland.

To the Chicken Hut for the gravy.

To the Limerick All-Ireland-winning hurling team for being absolute legends!

ABOUT THE ILLUSTRATOR

Fintan Taite is an award-winning illustrator, cartoonist and animator from Dublin. His unique work can be found in all areas of illustration, including children's publishing, animation, advertising and the corporate world.